#1
PLAY BALL!

Dean Hughes

Aladdin Paperbacks

First Aladdin Paperbacks edition March 1999

Copyright © 1999 by Dean Hughes

Aladdin Paperbacks
An imprint of Simon & Schuster
Children's Publishing Division
1230 Avenue of the Americas
New York, NY 10020

Also available in an Atheneum Books for Young Readers hardcover edition.

Designed by Amanda Foley

The text for this book was set in Caslon 540 Roman.

Printed and bound in the United States of America

10   9   8   7   6   5   4   3   2

The Library of Congress has cataloged the hardcover edition as follows:
Hughes, Dean, 1943–
Play ball! / by Dean Hughes.
p.   cm. — (Scrappers ; #1)
Summary: Having failed to get their applications in for the middle school summer baseball league, Robbie and Trent scramble to find a sponsor, a coach, and enough players to form their own team.
ISBN 0-689-81924-2 (hc)
[1. Baseball—Fiction.] I. Title. II. Series: Hughes, Dean, 1943–   Scrappers ; #1.
PZ7.H87312Sf   1999
[Fic]—dc21   98-14084
ISBN 0-689-81933-1 (pbk)

CHAPTER ONE

Robbie pulled up in front of Trent's house right on time. As he hit his brakes, his bike's back tire slid, leaving a nice stripe of black on the sidewalk.

When he looked up at Trent's house, he saw a head disappear from the front window. Two seconds later the door opened and Trent popped out. He grabbed his bike off the front lawn, and in moments the two boys were on their way at top speed.

"What team do you think we'll be on?" Trent called to Robbie.

"I don't know. I only have one prediction: starting at shortstop—Robbie Marquez!"

"Don't you care what team you play for?"

"Not really. As long as we're on the same team, it doesn't matter to me."

"Yeah. Same here."

In a few minutes the boys pulled up in front of the little building that housed the Wasatch City Recreation Department. It was next to the town park with its complex of baseball and softball diamonds. Beyond the park was Mount Timpanogos, part of the Wasatch Range of the Rocky Mountains, in Utah. Robbie could think of nothing better than summer days out on those fields playing shortstop. He had been waiting all spring for this.

The boys left their bikes in the rack out front and walked inside. Robbie couldn't help smiling, from sheer joy, as they stepped into the main office.

Mrs. Barker, whose husband managed the Safeway grocery store in town, was sitting at the desk. "Hello, boys," she said. "I suppose you want to know what teams you're on."

"Yes, ma'am," Robbie said. "We're supposed to be on the same team. That's what we put on our applications, anyway."

"You're the Marquez boy, aren't you?"

"Yeah. Robbie."

"And I'm Trent Lubak."

"Okay." She began to thumb through a pile

of applications. "J . . . K . . . L . . . Lubak, Lubak." She looked puzzled as she flipped the papers back and thumbed through again. Finally, she said, "I'm sorry, I don't see a Lubak or a Marquez here. Are you boys sure you turned in your applications?"

"Uh . . . I think so," Trent said.

"What do you mean, Trent!" Robbie said. "We filled them out together—on your kitchen table. You said you would take them in the next morning."

"Yeah, I remember. I'm just not sure that . . ."

"What?"

"I was going to have my mom do it—but I think maybe I forgot."

"Are you kidding? Trent!" But Robbie wasn't so much angry as he was shocked. No baseball this summer? He suddenly felt sick. "Mrs. Barker," he said, "are we too late now?"

"Technically, yes." She considered for a moment, and then she said, "We do have three other late applications. And those kids really want to play, too. Do you think there's any way you could find seven more players and make up a full team?"

"Six."

Everyone turned to see who had spoken. Wilson Love was standing just inside the office door, where he apparently had been listening. He was a huge kid and a pretty good athlete. He and Robbie had played baseball together the year before.

"Hi, Robbie," Wilson said. He walked to the desk. "I wasn't going to play this year. But there's nothing else to do." He looked at Mrs. Barker. "I still want to get on a team, if I can."

"Well, if you boys can find enough kids for a full team, we could still fit you in. I'll take the applications today, but I've got to have time to rework the schedule."

"By what time?"

She leaned back and thought. She was a big woman with round cheeks and a nice smile. "Two o'clock would have to be the latest," she said.

Robbie looked at Trent and Wilson. "Do you think we can find that many guys by then?"

Wilson shrugged. "We can give it a shot, I guess."

Robbie asked Mrs. Barker for six applications,

which she placed in a folder and handed to him.

"I can't believe I forgot," Trent said as the boys walked outside.

The truth was, Robbie had no trouble believing it. Trent was always forgetting things—like his homework. "Don't worry about it now," he told Trent. "We've got to find six players fast. What time is it now?"

Wilson looked at his watch. "Almost ten. We've got four hours."

"Why don't we each go home and start calling everyone we can think of," Robbie suggested.

But Trent said, "We know the same guys. Let's work together."

Actually, that was a better idea. But Robbie wanted to do the talking. Trent wouldn't push hard enough.

"I'm not going to do it on the phone," Wilson said. "I'm going to go strong-arm some of my friends—tell them they gotta come through for me." He laughed in his deep voice.

"Okay. Let's meet back here at one o'clock and see how we're doing." Robbie was feeling a little more hopeful now, but he was still worried.

He lived for baseball, read the sports pages, collected cards, memorized stats. He just couldn't miss a season of play.

At least the phone campaign started well. Right away Robbie got hold of a couple of kids he knew from his neighborhood—Martin Epting and Chad Corrigan. Martin and Chad were actually lousy at sports, but all Robbie needed for right now were guys willing to play—not superstars. He talked them both into signing up, and Trent took applications to them while Robbie stayed on the phone.

But Robbie picked up nothing but strikeouts after that. Everybody had a reason he couldn't play. By the time he and Trent headed back to the league office, they were praying that Wilson had found more guys than they had.

As Robbie and Trent pulled up to the office, Wilson yelled to them from the bleachers beside one of the softball diamonds where a team was practicing. As they approached him, he shook his head. "Sorry, guys. I only got one," he said.

"We got two," Trent told him. "And neither one of them is any good."

"I got a kid named Thurlow Coates," Wilson

said, "and he *is* good—if he'll show up. But I had to get his mom to put the pressure on him. He doesn't want to play."

"Why not?" Robbie wasn't sure he'd ever seen this kid.

"I don't know. Something is going on between him and his mom. They sound like they're mad at each other all the time."

"Yeah, well," Robbie said, "it won't matter either way if we can't find three more guys in the next hour." He sat down on the front row of the bleachers next to Wilson. "Okay, try to think of *anyone* we haven't asked." Trent sat next to the other two, and they all thought, but no one came up with a name.

Suddenly there was a voice behind them, up higher in the bleachers. "What are you doing, Katie?!" the girl yelled. "You missed your cutoff man!"

She had a voice like a diesel engine—rough and loud. Robbie glanced around in time to see her drop back to her seat. She turned to the girl next to her, and in a slightly lower voice said, "That's stupid to try to throw from the fence all the way to the plate."

"It was partly Cindy's fault," the other girl said. "She wasn't set up to take the relay. Our coach always said to get out there and show a target to the outfielder."

By now all three boys had turned around, and they were staring at the girls. Robbie had seen them around town. They were about his age, but he didn't really know them.

"I'm glad I'm not playing this year," the girl with the big voice said. "These teams are *rotten*."

Robbie glanced at Trent and Wilson, who were both nodding. "Then why don't you play baseball?" Robbie said. He stood up and faced the girls. When neither answered, he hiked up through the empty bleachers and stood in front of them.

"Who asked you to *eavesdrop* on our conversation?" the loudmouthed girl said.

Robbie laughed. "Hey, people on the East Coast could probably hear you."

"Take a leap, okay? Off these bleachers, for starters. We're trying to watch the practice."

"And not enjoying it. What grade are you in?"

"None of your business."

But the other girl said, "We'll be in seventh this fall. Why do you want to know?"

"You're the right age. Why don't you play in the city baseball league with us? We're trying to put a team together, and we need more players."

"Are all the rest of the players boys?"

"Yeah. So far."

"And jerks, like you three?"

Robbie smiled. "We're actually okay guys once you get to know us." He felt like adding, "unlike you," but he needed players—anyone who could sign an application. Even this loud-mouth.

"How come you're just putting a team to-gether now?"

"That's a long story. But Mrs. Barker told us we can still play if we find twelve players. We've got nine now. You two could get us to eleven."

Both girls looked like athletes. The girl with the loud voice was tall and strong, with short, dark hair. The other girl was smaller, but she looked wiry, even tough. She said, "We thought about playing baseball, but girls on those teams usually get stuck on the bench."

Robbie was taken by surprise. The girl sounded halfway interested. "Not on our team," he assured her. "We don't have a lot of hotshot players."

"Oh, great," the taller girl said. "Why do we want to play with a bunch of losers? Me and Tracy are *good*."

"Then you would probably be starters for us."

The girl broke into a laugh. "You'll say anything to get us to sign up."

Robbie smiled. "Hey, everything I've said is true."

The girls looked at each other. "Do you want to play, Gloria?" Tracy asked.

Gloria took a long look at Robbie, then glanced at the other two. "I'll tell you what," she said. "I'll fill out an application, so you'll have a better shot at making your deadline. But if I come to practice and you guys stink, then I'm outta there."

"Yeah. Same here," Tracy said. "And we're not putting up with any garbage about girls playing baseball."

"You've got it," Robbie said. "Everything will be fair. I promise."

So the girls filled out the applications. Their names were Gloria Gibbs and Tracy Matlock. They went to Valley View, the other middle school in town.

"So we need one more," Wilson said, as the boys walked back to their bikes. "And we're running out of time."

"Maybe we can ride through town and watch for guys our age," Trent said.

It wasn't much of a strategy, but it was better than any idea Robbie had. They wasted fifteen minutes that way, however, and had no luck. The situation was more than urgent.

"Okay, I know what we can do," Robbie finally said. It was an idea he had been hatching for a little while, but he had hardly dared to suggest it. Now he saw no other choice. He pulled out the last application from the folder.

Wilson looked over Robbie's shoulder to see what he was writing. "Who's that?"

"Tony Marquez, my cousin from Colorado. Maybe he's coming to stay with me this summer."

"What do you mean, 'maybe'?" Trent asked.

"Let's just say he would if he could. And this

will give us a total of twelve applications."

"Why can't he?" Wilson asked.

"Because I don't have a cousin named Tony in Colorado. I'm making him up."

"What do we do when he doesn't show?" Wilson asked.

"Look, we've got to get our team on that schedule. This will buy us some time. Then we can find someone else to take his place."

"We could get in trouble for this, Robbie."

"I know. But either we do this or we don't play."

"The worst thing they can do is kick us out," Wilson said, "and that's what happens anyway if we don't turn this in."

Trent shrugged and said, "Okay," but Robbie knew he didn't like the idea. Robbie didn't feel particularly good about it either. But he had to play, whatever it took.

Mrs. Barker seemed pleased when Robbie turned in the applications. She counted them and then congratulated the boys. "I'm amazed you could do it," she said. "Now . . . you need a sponsor and a coach."

"Doesn't the league take care of that?"

"No. We usually help you find coaches, but we don't have anyone right now. And the teams find their own sponsors to buy uniforms and equipment."

"Why didn't you tell us that before?"

She laughed. "I didn't want to discourage you."

Robbie couldn't believe it. "I guess you thought you'd wait and do that later," he said. She laughed again, but he didn't. "How much time do we have to find them?" he asked.

"I have to post a schedule by tomorrow at noon. I'll give you until six o'clock today—when the office closes."

"What does a sponsor have to do?"

Mrs. Barker handed Robbie a sheet of paper with the requirements on it. He scanned through it. The bottom line was, it could cost upwards of three hundred dollars.

Robbie took a deep breath. "All right," he said. "Thanks."

But he wasn't feeling very grateful as he walked out the door. He hadn't expected this new problem.

CHAPTER TWO

Robbie wondered whether it wasn't time to give up. He could see in his friends' faces that they were thinking the same thing. How could they find a coach and a sponsor at the last minute?

"I'll bet all the places that usually sponsor teams have already been asked," Wilson said. "McDonald's, Wendy's—places like that."

"Probably," Robbie agreed. "I guess we'll have to start on Main Street, and just ask people."

"We can't put all our time into that," Trent said. "We've got to find a coach, too, and that might be even harder."

Robbie saw Gloria and Tracy walking over from the softball diamond. Robbie had noticed before that Gloria was wearing a ratty old sweatshirt with the sleeves cut out. Now he saw that her jeans were torn at the knees and her sneakers were stained dark—as though covered with grease. She looked about half mad all the time, too. Tracy actually looked sort of cute, with her blond hair tied up in a ponytail, but the girl had acid in her voice. Both girls scared Robbie.

"So did you geniuses pull it off?" Gloria asked. "Do we have a team or not?"

"Yes and no," Wilson said. "We have enough players, but now we have to find a sponsor and a coach."

"You didn't mention that before."

"We didn't know that was part of the deal."

"I guess as long as you look dumb, you might as well be dumb."

Robbie came pretty close to telling Gloria to get lost. But he only said, "We'll try to look more like you in the future." He glanced down at her torn jeans and her grungy shoes.

"Don't start with me," Gloria said. "Not unless you're ready to finish what you start."

Robbie decided to let the whole thing go. "Do you know anyone who could sponsor us?" he asked. "We need to find some relative or friend—someone who will agree to it, quick, so we've got time to find a coach."

"Wait a minute," Tracy said. "How soon do you have to have all this?"

"By six."

"No way."

Gloria had her hands in her back pockets. "What exactly does a sponsor have to do?" she asked.

Robbie pulled the folded sheet from his back pocket and handed it to her.

Gloria studied it closely, and then she whistled. "Three hundred bucks. I don't know if my dad would do it."

"Does your dad have a business?" Trent asked.

"Yeah. A salvage yard. Out on the edge of town."

Robbie managed not to laugh, but Wilson couldn't hold back. "You mean, Jack's Scrap and Salvage, out on the old highway?"

Wilson was a lot bigger than Gloria, but she stepped right up to him. "Yeah. What about it?"

"Nothing. I was just wondering how we could get such a long name on our shirts."

Robbie stepped in between Gloria and Wilson. "Will he do it?"

"I don't know. It depends on what kind of mood he's in."

Robbie noticed Tracy shaking her head, as if to say, "You don't want to do this." But no one had a better idea.

"Let's go talk to him," Robbie said.

"Wait a minute." Gloria pointed her finger at Robbie's face. "I don't know if I can talk Dad into this, but there's one thing I do know. He is not going to back this up if he thinks I'm going to be sitting on the bench."

"We told you. You get a fair shot at a starting position, the same as anyone."

"What if I want to *pick* my position?"

Robbie saw trouble. "The coach should decide that," he said. He took a step back, but Gloria took another step forward.

"You don't have a coach. And you don't have a sponsor either, unless I can get you one. I'd think you might want to bargain a little at this point."

"What position do you want to play?"

"Shortstop."

Robbie had seen that one coming. He thought for a few seconds, and then he said,

"Well, I guess I don't blame you. You're probably worried that you wouldn't get the position if you had to compete for it . . . against a boy."

"Don't give me that. I can kick any boy's butt."

"Maybe." And now it was Robbie who stepped up close. "But I want to play shortstop, and I'm thinking I can beat you out in a fair try-out."

"Hey, you're on."

Wilson started to laugh, and then Tracy joined him. Gloria seemed to realize about then that she had just bargained away her deal. But she was obviously too proud to take anything back. "Let's just go talk to my dad," she said. "If we stand here all day, we won't ever have a team."

So all the kids got on their bikes, and on the way to the scrap yard, Tracy said, "Do any of you know Chester Carlton?"

No one responded.

"He's an old guy," Tracy said. "He lives in my neighborhood. He told me that he used to coach at the high school, and he even played pro ball in the minor leagues."

"Is he too old to coach?" Wilson asked.

"Probably. But we could ask."

"Okay," Robbie said. "This might work out."

Tracy was riding next to him, and she whispered, "Maybe. But be careful with Gloria's dad. Let her do the talking."

Ten minutes later Robbie stood facing the man, and he understood what Tracy had meant. Jack Gibbs was a very big man, with a pair of huge blue coveralls stretched over a stomach that would fill a hula hoop. And every inch of him was stained like Gloria's shoes.

"What now?" he asked Gloria, but for some reason, he stared straight at Robbie.

"Me and Tracy are going to play baseball with these guys this summer," Gloria began. "But we can't have a team if we can't get a sponsor."

"Don't look at me, little girl. I can't help you."

He rotated 180 degrees and began his retreat.

"Wait a minute, Dad. It won't cost all that much. We can probably find some cheap uniforms somewhere—and that's your biggest expense. And we could drive down to Salt Lake, to that used sports equipment place. We could probably—"

"How much?"

He was rotating again. When he came full circle, Gloria said, "A couple hundred. Something like that."

Mr. Gibbs smiled. "There's lots of guys in this town who've got more money than I do. Go talk to the man who owns the bowling alley."

"Dad, we need someone right now."

Wilson added, "Sir, you could have the name of your company on the uniforms. It's good advertising."

"I don't need advertising. I've got the only salvage yard within twenty miles of here."

"Dad, you could come to the games. Yell and cheer, call the umpire names—all that stuff."

Gloria had finally struck a chord. Mr. Gibbs grinned. "Who are you going to play against?" he asked.

"Other kids in town. Sixth- and seventh-graders."

"No. I mean, who else's names would be on the uniforms?"

Robbie said, "We don't know for sure. Businesses. Banks. Places like that."

"Would I get to pick a name for the team?"

"I guess," Robbie said. Now they were getting somewhere.

"I like 'Jack's Scrappers.' That's a good name." His big round face blossomed with satisfaction.

"That's the name you would want on our uniforms?" Robbie asked.

"That's right. And then I want you to kick the butts of all those kids playing for banks and downtown stores."

"Well, sure. Jack's Scrappers. We could be that."

Mr. Gibbs turned again. As he walked away, he said, "Sign me up, Gloria. But you better be scrappy. I'm not backing a bunch of pansies."

"We'll be tough as nails, sir," Wilson called to Mr. Gibbs's back.

As soon as her dad was gone Gloria said, "When we beat *nobody*, my dad will never let me hear the end of it."

"We'll worry about that when the time comes," Robbie said. "Now let's go see that old guy about being our coach."

Trent stood looking out over the scrap yard. "Jack's Scrappers?" he asked, with a tone of doubt.

"Hey, it's all right. It's just a name."

"So's the Buttheads, but that doesn't mean I want it on my shirt."

"Just don't worry about it," Robbie said, but he, too, was imagining all the flak they would take from other teams. Maybe it would be just as well if this Mr. Carlton turned them down.

But when the kids stood on the man's porch, and he did say no, Robbie felt as though all the air had been sucked right out of him. Maybe all their work was for nothing after all.

"Could we at least talk it over with you?" Robbie asked.

Chester Carlton was a white-haired, thin man. He chuckled softly. "Son, I'm seventy years old. I can't be running around on a baseball diamond anymore."

"I heard you played pro ball at one time," Robbie said.

"Well, yes. I did." He leaned against the door frame and nodded. "But I never made it to the majors. World War II came along, and I had to go. By the time I got back, I wasn't the ballplayer I'd been."

"You must have been playing when DiMaggio was around."

"Oh, yes. Him and Ted Williams. Hank Greenberg. All those great players. I played on the same team with Al Kaline, before he made it to the big leagues."

"Then you must have been in the Tigers' organization."

"That's right. How would you know that?"

"I have some of Kaline's cards. I know he won the American League batting championship some time in the fifties. He and Harvey Kuenn were on the same team. They were both great hitters."

"That's right. And I'll tell you, they were players who would get down and get some dirt on their uniforms. None of this fancy-pants stuff you see now, with all the multimillion-dollar contracts."

"They were scrappers," Robbie said. He glanced at Gloria, who—for the first time all day—smiled just a little.

"Do you kids want to come in for a little bit?" Mr. Carlton asked.

"Sure," Robbie said, and he led the way.

And then, for twenty minutes, Robbie and Mr. Carlton talked about baseball in the forties and fifties. Mr. Carlton had more firsthand knowledge, but when it came to statistics, Robbie was way ahead of him. And Mr. Carlton was obviously impressed. Finally, he asked, "How in the world do you know all this stuff?"

"I love baseball, sir. I read about it all the time. I collect baseball cards. I watch games on TV. I go down to see the Salt Lake Buzz whenever I can. It's the biggest thing in my life."

"Can you play the game, or just talk about it?" Gloria laughed.

"Well . . . I play all right. But I've got a lot to learn. And the trouble is, if we don't come up with a coach by six o'clock, we won't have a team."

"Wait a minute. How did that come about?"

So Robbie told him the story while the other kids filled in a few of the details. Mr. Carlton listened and asked questions. Finally, he said, "That's a shame. Do all you kids feel the same way about baseball as Robbie here?"

"I don't know all those numbers, like him,"

Gloria said, "but I can play circles around any girl *or* boy around here."

Mr. Carlton laughed. And Robbie could see that he was thinking things over. Then he asked the right question. "So what's the name of this team?"

"The Scrappers, sir. We're tough. We're going to play ball the old-fashioned way."

Robbie knew he was blowing smoke, but he liked the look he saw on Mr. Carlton's face. "I like that," he said. "I really like that."

"Come and coach us then. We need someone who really knows the game."

Mr. Carlton laughed. "You're a sneaky kid, you know that?" he said. "You've known what you were up to this whole time."

"We need a coach, sir. I'm ready to do anything."

"If some kid's mom had agreed to coach, you would have taken her, just as quick. Right?"

"Well . . . yeah. But only because we want to play so bad."

Mr. Carlton nodded. He ran his fingers through his thin hair. He folded his arms and looked off at the far wall. Then, finally, he said,

"Well, all right. But you better be a bunch of scrappers, for real. The only way I coach is if you give the game everything you've got."

"We will," Wilson said. And all the other kids agreed.

"All right. First practice is tomorrow at eight in the morning, before it gets too hot. Will you be up in time?"

"Sure."

So the Scrappers were born, and Robbie was happy. Sort of. In the back of his mind was a very big worry. What was he going to do about Tony Marquez, his nonexistent cousin?

CHAPTER THREE

On the following morning Coach Carlton had all the kids sit down on the grass before he started practice. He called out the names on his roster so that he could put names with faces.

Robbie had tried the night before to find someone else who wanted to play. He thought he could tell Mrs. Barker that his cousin had cancelled his visit but that he had found a replacement. The only trouble was, he couldn't find anyone.

Robbie had never told so many lies in his life. And this morning he told another one. He claimed his cousin hadn't arrived from Colorado yet, but he would be getting in any time.

There was another problem. Thurlow Coates hadn't shown up. Robbie didn't know what the league would do if the team had a dropout already.

Once Robbie saw the whole team, his worries only grew. A guy named Jeremy Lim looked way too small for a middle school league. And another guy Robbie knew from school, Adam Pfitzer, acted like he had walked into a wall; he was moving, but he looked a little dazed. Still, that was better than the kid named Ollie Allman. He was a tall, gawky-looking kid who kept talking to himself while the coach was calling the roll. Chad and Martin, too, were talking to each other, hardly paying any attention to the coach.

What a season! Some of the guys were strange; the girls were scary; one guy didn't want to play; and one didn't exist.

"Robbie tells me that Tony will be here soon," the coach announced to all the players. "But where's the Coates boy?"

"He couldn't make it today," Wilson said.

The coach shook his head. "We gotta have everyone here," he said. "We need to start feeling like a team. I also need an assistant coach. Maybe one of your dads."

Robbie thought of his own father. Mr. Marquez hardly knew which end of a bat to grip. Soccer had been his game when he was a boy. He was a busy man, too, especially in the summer, operating his own cement contracting business.

"Are any of your dads willing to help me? Or maybe one of your mothers?"

Robbie's mom actually knew more about baseball, but she was busy, too. She worked as an accountant and then came home and kept her husband's books besides.

Robbie glanced around. For a moment his heart almost quit on him. Gloria shifted a little, and he thought she was going to raise her hand. That's all the Scrappers needed: Jack Gibbs for an assistant coach.

But not a single hand went up.

"Well, okay. But everyone go home and talk to your parents—or a big brother or sister. See if you can find someone interested." The coach looked down at his clipboard. "And what about uniforms?" he asked. "What's our sponsor doing about that?"

Coach Carlton definitely needed a uniform

himself. He had on a shirt from his high school coaching days, some old-fashioned reddish-colored dress pants, and a pair of high-top sneakers. He was a good guy, but he looked mighty weird.

Gloria sat up straight. "My dad said everyone will have to wear shorts or jeans, or whatever they want," she said. "He's only going to buy shirts. And I'm not sure how fast we'll have them."

Coach Carlton had plenty of wrinkles around his eyes, and they all seemed to get a little tighter at that point. "We need to *look* like a team, Gloria. I'll call your dad and tell him we need something decent—and right away. I brought some bats and balls I had around the house for today. But we need equipment, too. Including catcher's gear."

"Well . . . okay," Gloria said. "But don't call my dad. I better deal with him myself."

"I spoke to Mrs. Barker this morning," Coach Carlton said. "We're scheduled to play a team called the Whirlwinds on Friday. Gloria, see if your dad can have something for us by then."

Gloria nodded, but she made no promises.

"By the way, it's an evening game. Six o'clock. Everybody, let your parents know. We want to get all the support we can."

At the announcement of an evening game, there was a bit of chatter among the kids. As the sun went down they'd put on the lights, and playing under the lights always made Robbie feel like a major-leaguer.

"We've got a lot of work to do by then. I've got to see what you can do. Let's start with batting practice. If you're not up or on deck, get out in the field somewhere. Tracy, grab a bat. You, too, Robbie. Got any catchers on this team?"

No hands went up.

"Well, okay. Wilson, you're big as a backstop. Try your hand at catching, and I'll pitch for now."

The coach grabbed a bag of baseballs and walked to the pitcher's mound. Tracy and Robbie went to the fence on the third base side of the plate where a number of bats were lined up—all of them wooden. Robbie liked the solid click of a wooden bat meeting a baseball better than the ringing sound aluminum bats made.

He and Tracy swung a few of the bats, and

each picked one out. Wilson didn't have a catcher's mitt, just a regular glove, but he walked over and set up behind the plate.

"Ladies first," Robbie said to Tracy.

"What's that supposed to mean?" she shot back.

"*Nothing!* I was just being nice."

Tracy seemed rather pleased with herself, probably for making Robbie flinch.

"Batter up!" the coach was yelling. Tracy walked to the batter's box.

Coach Carlton threw a couple of easy pitches over the plate, and Tracy slapped them both into left field. Then she yelled, "Go ahead, Coach. Bring some heat."

Coach smiled, and then he popped one pretty hard. Robbie was surprised to see someone his age throw that hard. Tracy was caught off guard and fouled the first pitch off. But she was ready the next time and hit a long fly into center field.

Robbie was impressed with her power.

"You've got a nice, natural swing, Tracy," the coach told her. "But don't try to pull everything. You're stepping too much toward left field—and swinging too hard. Try striding straight ahead, and just go for line drives. I'm going to throw the ball a little outside, and you try to hit it to the right."

The coach put the ball where he promised, but it took Tracy a few tries to get used to her new stride. She hit some weak grounders before she finally drove one to the right side.

"All right," the coach said. "That's the idea." And then, as Tracy walked away from the plate, he added, "Tracy, you're going to get a lot of hits. You'll be a big help to us."

As Tracy walked past Robbie, he said, "It looks like the coach is going to give you girls a fair chance."

"Yeah. Maybe so," she said. "And I gotta say this: he knows what he's talking about."

That's exactly what Robbie was thinking, and that gave him some reason for hope.

But when Robbie batted, he didn't do quite so well. He knew he was trying a little too hard. But the coach made some corrections in his stance, and Robbie felt the difference immediately.

That was the good news. The bad news was

out on the field. Jeremy Lim kept taking off
after every fly, but he always seemed to start the
wrong way or overrun the ball. The kid was fast,
but he was zipping around all over the place and
catching nothing.

At least he was working hard. Martin Epting
and Chad Corrigan were standing in short left
field, talking to each other. Adam was standing
on top of second base, waiting but never moving. Ollie had decided to back up the coach and
catch the balls as they came flying back from the
fielders, but he was mumbling again—to himself. Trent was probably the best outfielder, but
so far he had dropped about half of the balls that
had come his way.

And, of course, Gloria had settled into the
shortstop position, like she thought she owned it.

Crack! Robbie finally caught one in the sweet
part of his bat. The ball shot toward right center.

Jeremy probably had a shot at catching it, but
he had started in and then had had to reverse
himself and go deep. The ball dropped in and
rolled almost to the fence.

"Nice shot!" the coach yelled.

Robbie liked that. And as he watched some

of the other kids bat, he thought he saw some fair talent. Everyone seemed to get better, too, as the coach worked with them. True, Wilson looked all wrong, and he swung and missed a lot. But when he connected, he really crunched the ball. He hit a couple over the fence.

So, maybe . . . just maybe . . . the Scrappers were going to be able to score a few runs. Maybe they could even win some games—if they could get anybody out.

When Gloria came up to bat, Robbie's hopes took another leap. The girl cracked out one line drive after another.

When everyone had hit, the coach called them all together at the mound. He was rolling and massaging his shoulder to get the kinks out. "All right, not bad at all. You kids all need some work, but I feel good about what I'm seeing. Let's take some fielding practice now. Wilson, stay behind the plate. Who wants to be a pitcher?"

Adam raised his hand.

"Okay. You look like a pitcher, with those long arms. Do you throw right or left?"

"Left."

"Oh, that's good. Anyone else?"

For a time, no other hands went up, but finally Ollie said, "I've pitched before, but I don't like to do it. I get too nervous."

"Well, we'll work on that. I'd like to see you give it a try. You and Adam can also trade off at first base. You're both tall enough to make the long stretch."

"I've done some pitching, too," Gloria said. "In fact, I've watched Adam pitch, and I'm a lot better than him. But I'd rather play shortstop. I think that's where I can help the team the most."

Coach Carlton smiled, showing his blunt, worn teeth. "You let me decide where you'll help us the most. But I'm glad to know where you'd like to be."

He gave everyone else the same chance. Jeremy, Trent, Martin, and Chad all said they wanted to play outfield. Tracy said she liked second base.

When the coach asked Robbie, he said, "Shortstop."

"What about third base?" the coach said.

"I like shortstop."

"Okay. We'll try you and Gloria both in that spot, but one of you will probably end up at third. For right now, let's see Ollie at first, Gloria at short, and Robbie at third. Adam, I'll swap you in for Ollie, but I don't want a pitcher out there right now. Trent, why don't you try left. Jeremy, center. And, Martin, right. Chad, you take turns with Martin for now."

All the kids turned to take their positions.

"Listen, everybody," the coach said, "I'm not making any decisions today. There's another practice before the game. And we still need to see what Thurlow and Tony can do. So get out there and do your best—and have a good time. Let's go."

Gloria gave Robbie a look as she walked to short. Robbie knew she was trying to tell him that the butt kicking was about to start. He tried to look confident himself as he walked toward third base.

Coach Carlton started by hitting fly balls to the outfield and pop-ups to the infield. But that was not a beautiful sight. Robbie saw some pretty good speed, but not nearly enough skill. Then the coach hit grounders to the infield. Tracy looked like a solid second baseman. Ollie and Adam were both fairly decent first basemen, and even though Robbie hated to admit it, Gloria played well at short.

He still thought he was better though.

True, he booted a couple, and he missed on some of his throws, but he wasn't used to third base.

When practice finally ended, Gloria walked over to him. "Hey, you're better than I thought you'd be," she said.

Since she was being nice for once, he replied, "Yeah, well, you are, too."

"I know. I'm better than you. But still, you're not bad."

Robbie shook his head, and then he turned to walk away.

"Hey, I was just kidding."

"What?"

"I was just giving you a hard time. You are pretty good."

"But you do think you're better. Right?"

She grinned. "Well, yeah. But you think

you're better than me, don't you?"

"Sure."

Now she laughed. "How come boys are always wrong?" she said, and then she walked away. Robbie let her go.

On Robbie's way home, he stopped by his mom's office. "Mom," he told her, "there's still one thing we need. An assistant coach. Do you think you could do that?"

Her eyes got huge. And just then the phone on her desk rang. By the time she was off the phone, she had her answer, too. "Oh, honey, I just couldn't."

Actually, that was the answer Robbie expected, maybe even wanted; but he felt like he had to do what the coach had requested and at least ask.

"But, Robbie, if no one else can, check back with me. I'm proud of you. You've worked so hard to get this team together. I wouldn't want to let it fail now."

"Oh, don't worry. It won't. We don't have to have an assistant. The coach just wants one."

"Still—let me know. I don't want to let you down."

When Robbie left, those were the words on his mind. Those, and her comment about how proud she was of him. Robbie found himself wondering whether she would say that if she knew the whole story—and he didn't like the answer that came to mind.

CHAPTER FOUR

Robbie went home and got on the phone again. He called everyone he could think of, even guys he had called before. But everyone had an excuse. Swimming lessons. Summer camp. Family trips. Allergies. Robbie heard it all. He could tell that half of the kids just didn't like baseball, which drove him crazy.

Once he thought he had a guy—Ricky Ingleby—talked into playing, and he spent half the evening keeping the pressure on. But Ricky's mother made him choose between baseball and a community play he was supposed to be in. And Ricky chose the play. Robbie wanted to kill him.

What it all came down to was that Robbie showed up at practice the next day without another player—and he had to tell another lie. "Well, see," he told the coach, "Tony's family got delayed. But I think they're leaving from Colorado today. Maybe they'll get here tonight . . . or something."

At least Wilson had better news. Thurlow would come today—for sure.

But when it was time for the practice to start, Thurlow still hadn't shown. Wilson had to make up excuses of his own.

"I talked to the league president," Coach Carlton told the players, "and he said twelve is the absolute minimum. Some teams have fifteen or sixteen."

"I don't see why," Gloria said. "We only need nine."

"That's what I told Mr. Ahern. But he said kids take off on vacations and things. A team needs quite a few subs. If you start with nine, what do you do when players get hurt or get worn out in the heat?"

"Tell them not to be crybabies," Gloria whispered. With her voice, however, everyone heard.

"What if only ten or eleven show up to a game?" Robbie asked.

"That's a problem. They want twelve. Mr. Ahern told me he'd like to see us recruit two or three more, just to be sure we don't run short sometimes. I sure hope this cousin of yours gets here before tomorrow night."

"I'm pretty sure he will," Robbie said, softly. "I'll try to find some other kids, too."

More pressure. Robbie just wished he could tell the truth and get it over with. All this worry was making his stomach ache.

"But there's more to it than that," the coach said. "Baseball is all about teamwork. If a kid is missing practice, he's not getting to know the other players. In the long run, that just won't work."

"I'll get Thurlow here," Wilson said. "I promise."

Practice went about the same as the day before, except that Robbie played shortstop, and the coach tried Gloria at third. She did a good job, too. But Robbie was comfortable at short and he showed it. By the end of practice, he was almost sure he had nailed down the position.

"The coach has to make a hard choice," Gloria told him. "I'm better than you at third. But I'm also better at short. It's too bad I can't play both positions."

Robbie rolled his eyes and turned to walk away.

But Gloria said, "Hey, Robbie, what's your problem? When I say stuff like that, you're supposed to come back at me. Tell me you're better than I am."

"I don't see why. I don't need someone putting me down all the time."

"Oh, brother," Gloria said. "What do you want from me? A valentine, with lots of little hearts on it?"

That was not exactly what Robbie had in mind.

What he did need were some new recruits. But he had no more luck that night. He got almost frantic, calling kids—girls and boys both—that he knew didn't even play sports. He got so frustrated he was almost rude to some of them, but he still got nowhere.

All the next day he waited for the balloon to pop. He tried to convince his parents that they didn't have to go to the game that night, but they said they wanted to. Robbie knew that if the coach happened to ask Robbie's parents about his cousin, he was a dead man.

So as he rode to the game with his parents and his little sister, Maria, he was expecting disaster: a big embarrassment, followed by the end of his baseball season—and a whole lot of people upset with him.

"You seem a lot more nervous this year, Robbie," his dad said. "Is it this whole business about which position you'll play?"

"I guess so."

But Maria giggled, and then she said, "He doesn't want a *girl* to be better than him. But I think she is."

"That's enough of that, Maria," his mom said. "From what I hear, the Gibbs girl can really play. But Robbie can, too. A coach just has to decide who's best suited to play in certain positions."

"Especially if the girl is better," Maria said.

Normally, Robbie would have defended himself, but he was in no mood for that tonight. He looked out the window and let Maria laugh. He was thinking about facing the coach one more time, and telling him that Tony still hadn't arrived.

But as it turned out, the coach only said, "I

was afraid of that. I talked to the Whirlwinds' coach, and he said that he doesn't care if we play without the full twelve."

Robbie took a deep breath of relief. He had bought a little more time again. If nothing else, he would get to play one game.

When Wilson arrived on his bike, he took one look at Robbie and began shaking his head. "I thought I had Thurlow this time," he said. "His mom made him come with me. But he got halfway here and said, 'See you around, sucker,' and he took off."

Robbie thought for a minute, and then he said, "Look, let's play this game—for the fun of it—and then let's tell the coach the truth."

"That'll be the end of the team, Robbie."

"I know. But what else can we do?"

Wilson had no answer for that.

That was bad, but what made it worse was that Robbie could see the coach's excitement when he called the kids together. The team was obviously starting to mean a lot to him.

But the worst thing of all happened when the coach announced the lineup. Robbie was batting third and playing shortstop. It was perfect:

exactly what he had dreamed about.

True, Jack Gibbs hadn't come through with any equipment or uniforms yet. True, the boys on the Whirlwinds started right off calling the Scrappers the "scrap heap." True, Adam showed up without his glove and said, "Oh, yeah. I forgot." And, true, Jeremy was so hyped up he couldn't hold still, while Chad, on the other hand, hardly moved at all. And also true that Gloria told him the coach was putting her on third base because her arm was stronger—which it probably was.

But even with all that, he was still the third batter and the shortstop. And the Scrappers had some pretty good potential and a good coach. It was terrible to think their first game could also be their last.

The Scrappers were the home team that evening, so they would be taking the field first. The coach told them, "This is it, kids. Remember what we've been learning. Concentrate. Talk to one another. And have a good time. It's a great game."

The players gathered around in a circle and put their hands together. "One, two, three, GO

SCRAPPERS!" they shouted. Then they fanned out to their positions around the field.

The Whirlwinds' first batter stepped into the box. Everyone, on both sides—and up in the bleachers—was talking it up, and Robbie's heart was racing.

Adam must have been all pumped up, too. He wound up and delivered, way high. And the next pitch was worse. He never got a pitch close to the strike zone; the batter walked on four pitches.

"That's okay, Adam," Robbie yelled, and he pounded his fist into his glove. "The play's at second. Let's get this one."

Gloria was yelling the same kind of stuff, and Tracy was shouting, "Hey, Adam, this kid can't hit. Smoke it by him."

"Relax, Adam," the coach kept saying. "Just throw strikes. You can do it."

Adam did let up, but he aimed the ball and floated a pitch over the plate. The batter smacked it to shallow center. Jeremy got a quick jump on it, raced forward, reached down, and made a good catch at his knees.

Robbie could hardly believe it, but he

shouted, "All right, Jeremy! Great catch!"

Jeremy smiled and nodded. But the kid seemed surprised himself.

All the Scrappers were psyched now and yelling their heads off. Robbie loved it.

But the next batter stepped up, took a couple of outside pitches, and then drove the ball over Tracy's head. Martin ran hard, but he was out of control, and the ball skipped past him. He spun around and chased after it, but by the time he came up with it, the runner from first had already scored and the hitter was rounding second, heading for third.

Martin should have tossed the ball to Tracy, the cutoff, but instead he let fly with a wild throw toward third. It was way off line, and Gloria had to run to the fence to chase it down. Adam hadn't thought to back her up.

Another run scored.

Robbie didn't want to drop his head, so he looked straight into the sky and took a deep breath. He could hear all the Whirlwinds players shouting about the "piece of scrap" out in right field. And Gloria was kicking in the dirt and mumbling about "that idiot out there."

Unfortunately, the game kept going the same way for a time. The Scrappers had some surprisingly good moments and some solid hitting. They were scoring pretty well. But every time things started to look up, someone would make a big error—or mental mistake—and the Whirlwinds would pick up some more runs.

But then, Robbie couldn't complain about his teammates. He made two crucial errors himself, and he struck out once with runners on second and third.

When the game reached the top of the sixth, the score was 13 to 7.

Adam's first pitch of the inning tailed away from the batter, a lefty. The guy smacked it in the hole between Robbie and Gloria. Both broke for it, but Gloria got there first. She knocked the ball down but couldn't pick it up in time to make the throw.

Gloria kicked at the dirt again, now angry with herself. She mumbled something about playing the ball wrong. "I don't know how to play third," she said. "The ball gets here too quick."

Robbie was surprised she would admit that much. The fact was, Gloria was having a good game. She had made some great stops, and she could handle the long throw to first.

The frustration continued. Adam walked the next batter. He had been walking people all night long. And this was not like Little League. In this league a pitcher had to have something on the ball, or someone would lose it for him over the fence.

Robbie backed up a little and set himself. The next batter was a guy Robbie had played against before: Chuck Kenny. He was good at every sport he played. But he was a mouthy kid.

Chuck slapped the first pitch up the middle. Robbie dug hard, got in front of the ball, and fielded it cleanly. There was no chance for a play at third, but he tossed the ball to Tracy, who was ready at second. She tried to pivot and throw back to first, but she couldn't get much power on the throw. The runner was safe at first.

It was a good play, and Gloria told Robbie so. So did Trent, who was yelling from left field. What occurred to Robbie was that he wasn't hearing much from anyone else. Robbie had the feeling that the kids were giving up, figuring this game was lost.

Chuck started working on Adam immediately. "We'll take some more walks, Adam," he
yelled. "Just keep serving them up." And then
he yelled to the next batter, "No pitcher, Russ!
No pitcher! Let him walk you!"

Russ stepped into the batter's box. He had a
funny-looking stance, with his bat cocked too
high, but he wasn't looking for a walk. He connected on the first pitch and pulled a grounder
up the third base line.

Gloria scooped it up, looked the runner on third
back, and then fired to second for another out.

Tracy waited for Chuck as he pulled up short
of the bag. "Why did you stop? I wanted to flat-
ten you," she said.

"Oh, so you think you're bad, do you?" he
sniped back at her. "If you weren't a girl, I'd
show you who's bad around here."

"Bring it on, skinny. I'll duke it out with you,
anytime." Tracy strode toward him, obviously
not frightened at all.

Instantly, the umpire in the field charged toward the two, got between them, and said,
"Watch yourselves, kids. We have an automatic
suspension for fighting."

"This guy is out," Tracy said. "Tell him to get off my field and shut his big mouth."

Chuck did backpedal toward his dugout, but he grinned as he called out, "Maybe I'm out, but check the score."

For the first time all night, Ollie said something—other than to himself. "Get out of here," he yelled. And from right field, Chad, who was now playing for Martin, yelled, "Keep your mouth shut, Chuck. This game ain't over yet."

The next batter lifted a little fly into left field, and Trent came up to make a catch for the third out. Robbie was glad to get out of the inning without giving up any runs, but he was even happier to see the Scrappers seeming to come back to life.

Coach Carlton noticed it, too. He walked over to the fenced-in area used as a dugout. "Hey, I like what I'm seeing out there now. But let's not start mouthing off with those kids. Let's show them on the field what we can do."

"We can still win this game," Gloria bellowed.

"That's right," the coach said, and he grinned. "We're only down by six runs. Chad, go out there and get a hit. Let's get us a rally going."

CHAPTER FIVE

Chad was the last batter in the lineup. And for good reason. The kid was a disaster at the plate. At practice the coach had tried everything, but Chad still looked like a little kid who had just picked up a bat for the first time.

The Scrappers needed to get something going this inning, but Robbie didn't hold out much hope for a good start.

"This kid can't hit!" Chuck was screaming to the outfielders. "Move up."

"Don't let him bother you," Wilson shouted to Chad. But then he yelled, "Make him pitch to you. Don't swing at anything bad."

Robbie knew what Wilson was really thinking: hold out for a walk.

Chad did let the first two pitches go by for balls, and all the Scrappers yelled for him to keep taking. But on the next pitch Chad started to swing, then changed his mind and tried to hold up. The ball hit his bat and looped toward the right side.

Chuck was playing too close to the bag, leaving a big hole, and the ball dropped in beyond the reach of the second baseman.

Chad ran hard and—for some reason—slid into first. Maybe he didn't know that he could overrun the bag. But then, he had probably never gotten that far before.

Chad got up and dusted himself off, and then he stood next to Chuck, with one foot on the base and a huge smile on his face. He waved to his parents, who were both screaming that he was the greatest. Chuck's mouth was going, and Robbie was sure that he was telling Chad that he had lucked out. But Chad didn't seem to care.

Jeremy—at the top of the batting order—was up next. He had a quick bat, but he wasn't very careful about what he swung at. This time he took a swipe at a low pitch and knocked a slow roller toward third. The third baseman charged the ball and made a decent throw, but Jeremy was too fast. He beat the throw on a close play.

The excitement was starting to build. "Let's keep it going," everyone was yelling. "We can still beat these guys."

With runners at first and second, Adam came up. He was not a bad hitter, even though he seemed not to be paying much attention most of the time. Without ever swinging, he worked the count to 3 and 2—building the Scrappers' hopes even higher—but then he finally swung. And missed.

Robbie came up with two men on and one away. He was in a tough position. If he got on base, he would keep things going. But if he didn't, even if there was still another out, he would pretty much kill the rally. He glanced at his parents. His mom waved her fist and yelled, "Come on, Robbie. You can do it!" His dad nodded at him, confidently.

Robbie told himself all the right things: *Watch the ball. Don't swing at bad pitches. Swing level. Don't try to kill it.*

The first two pitches were outside, and Robbie let them go by. Then, on the third pitch, he got one over the plate. He took a hard swing and got pretty good wood, but the ball bounced toward Chuck, at first. It looked like a sure out, but then the ball took a wild bounce over Chuck's head. It rolled into right field for a single.

Chad scored from second, and Jeremy raced around second and stopped at third. Chuck, of course, was furious. He pounded his glove and muttered to himself. Robbie thought of some things he could say to the guy, but it was more fun just to listen to him whine.

Wilson was up next. Everything the guy did looked wrong, and he swung way too hard. But when he got hold of one, look out. He had already hit a homer in the third inning.

The Whirlwinds' pitcher seemed a little rattled now. He threw a couple of high pitches—even too high for Wilson to swing at—and then forced one into the strike zone. Wilson almost came out of his shoes he swung so hard, and he drove the ball on a line, straight at the left field fence.

Robbie leaped into the air when he saw the ball take off. "Here we go!" he shouted. The ball cleared the fence and was still traveling on a flat line.

Robbie chugged around the bases, crossed the plate, and then waited with the rest of his teammates as Wilson loped around the bases. Everyone mobbed him at home plate.

The score was 13 to 11 now. The Scrappers really did have a shot.

"Come on, Trent," everyone was yelling. "Keep it going!"

And he did. Trent hit a solid shot over the second baseman's head. It dropped in for a single.

Gloria came up next. As she stepped into the box, the lights came on. Robbie hadn't noticed how dark it had become until the field was lit up. It seemed like a sign. He felt it in his bones: The Scrappers were going to pull this game out.

Trent took a healthy lead away from the bag as the pitcher wound up. The pitch was fat, and Gloria smacked it. Trent took off hard for second, but he underestimated the speed of the center fielder. Trent was ready to round second when the Whirlwind player reached up and snagged the ball.

Trent spun around and dug back toward first,

but he had no chance. The throw was there for the double play.

And that was the end of the rally.

Robbie couldn't believe it. The big comeback bid was over. He yelled to everyone that the game wasn't over, that the Scrappers still had another chance in the bottom of the seventh.

But something seemed to go out of the players. They said all the right things, but they didn't run onto the field with much fire. Then Adam started having more trouble getting the ball over the plate. It was all downhill from there. The Whirlwinds scored three runs, all on walks and errors, and the Scrappers couldn't get anything going in the bottom of the seventh. They lost the game 16 to 11.

The coach gave a nice little speech after the game. "You kids showed me some potential tonight," he said. "We can be a good team. We just need to work harder than the other teams in the league. And we need to stop the kind of mental errors we made tonight. But that's something we can do."

That actually sounded pretty exciting to

Robbie, but the other reality was now returning. Once his lie was revealed, this probably would be the last game the Scrappers would play anyway.

Robbie heard Gloria mumble, "We need to get rid of half of these kids. I know about five girls who are better than Martin and Chad."

Robbie leaned toward her and whispered, "Can you get any of them to play for us?"

"What?"

But the coach was finishing his little pep talk. "Let's get together tomorrow morning early. We have a lot of things we have to work on before we play our next game." Then he looked at Robbie. "Are we going to have enough players?" he asked.

"I don't know . . . for sure." This was the first time he had ever admitted that much, and everyone suddenly fell silent. Robbie knew he should admit the whole truth, as he had planned, but he hated to disappoint everyone.

"Come on, kids, we've got to find a couple more players," the coach said, and Robbie could tell it mattered to him.

Robbie made more promises to try, but as

soon as the meeting broke up, he turned to Gloria. "What about it?" he said. "Can you get any of those girls you say are better?"

"They're all playing softball."

But Tracy said, "Maybe we can talk Cindy into playing for us."

Gloria shrugged. "Maybe," she said. "She's good friends with us. Maybe we can talk her into it."

"Okay. Go talk to her right now. And I'll go with Wilson. We'll see if there's some way to get Thurlow here."

So the girls took off, and, although it was getting dark, Robbie and Wilson rode their bikes to Thurlow's house. Mrs. Coates answered the door. "Well, hello, Wilson," she said.

"Hello," Wilson said. "Is Thurlow here?"

"Sure. He just came in. He wouldn't say if you kids won or lost. How did it turn out?"

"We lost," Wilson said, but he didn't mention that Thurlow hadn't been there.

"Oh, that's too bad. Come on in, and I'll get Thurlow. Who's this you've got with you?"

"Robbie Marquez. He's on our team."

Mrs. Coates was a big woman, not heavy, but

tall and sturdy. "Hello. I'm Wanda Coates," she said. And then she yelled to Thurlow, "Come on in here, son. Some of your teammates are here to see you."

Robbie heard a groan from a back room. Mrs. Coates shook her head, and then she said, "Sit down, boys. I'll go get you something cold to drink." She disappeared into the kitchen.

After a minute or two, a tall guy with big shoulders—built like his mom—appeared. Robbie suddenly remembered seeing this guy play in a game the year before. He *had* been amazing, just like Wilson had said.

"Hey, Wilson," Thurlow said. Then he looked at Robbie, and he spoke softly. "I know what you're here to say, but I'm not playing. Just don't tell my mom."

"But we need you," Robbie pleaded.

"Forget it," he whispered. "I'm not interested."

"Why not?"

"Hey, I never did want to play. Wilson talked me into signing up so you guys would have enough applications."

"Don't you like baseball?"

"No. I don't."

But that couldn't be true. Robbie had seen how good he was.

About then Mrs. Coates appeared with three glasses of soda on a tray. "What are you boys whispering about?" she asked. And then she handed the sodas to the boys.

"Nothing," Thurlow said. "These guys just stopped by to tell me something. They have to go now."

But Wilson said, "He didn't play tonight, Mrs. Coates. He got halfway to the game and took off. That's one of the big reasons we lost."

"Thanks a lot," Thurlow growled, and he dropped into a big chair.

Mrs. Coates stood with her hands on her hips, staring at him. Finally, she said, "What's this all about, Thurlow?"

"I don't want to play. I told you that."

Robbie figured it was time to turn the heat up a little. "Mrs. Coates," he said, "if he doesn't play for us, we don't have enough players. We'll have to drop from the league—and none of us will get to play."

Mrs. Coates looked at Thurlow again. "The

first thing I want to know is where you've been all evening if you didn't play ball."

Thurlow shrugged. "Just hanging out with my friends," he said. Mrs. Coates had fire in her eyes, but she took a long breath, and then she said, "Wilson and Robbie, sit down. We need to talk."

"There's nothing to talk about," Thurlow said. "I'm not playing."

"Don't you talk that way to me. I'm your mother."

Thurlow set his drink down, and then he crossed his arms and stared straight ahead. He didn't say a word, but Robbie could see that a contest of wills was coming.

"Thurlow is the best ballplayer in this town—at least for his age," Mrs. Coates said. "But he's mad at me. He thinks he's getting back at me if he doesn't play."

"That's not it," Thurlow said. "My sport is basketball. I want to work on it year-round."

"Here's what's really going on," Mrs. Coates said. "Thurlow let his grades go down the drain last fall, during football season. So I told him he couldn't go out for basketball until he got them up. I wouldn't sign the permission slip, and that made him mad."

"Hey, I got my grades up."

"Yes, you did. And I'm proud of you for that. And if you keep them up, you can play basketball next year. But there's no reason not to play baseball in the summer. You're just being stubborn—to spite me."

"No way. That's not it."

"Then what is it?"

"You try to tell me what friends I can have and which ones you want me to stay away from. I don't like that. I got a right to choose. So I'm doing what I want to do this summer."

Mrs. Coates sat for quite some time, and Robbie thought maybe she had lost the battle, but when she finally spoke, it was with authority. "You signed up for baseball, Thurlow. When you did that, you made a promise to these boys. Now they're about to miss out on a whole season, just because of you. That's not right."

"It's not my fault. Wilson begged me to sign. He had to have some names in by two that day. That's the only reason I said I would do it."

"You still signed. And you're still going to

play. And you're not going to sneak off again, because I'm going to every game—every practice if I have to—just to make sure you're there."

Robbie suddenly realized what an opportunity he had. "Mrs. Coates," he said, "we need an assistant coach. If you love baseball, you'd be great at it."

"I like to watch it, and I even played a little softball in high school, but I'm no coach."

"We've got a good coach. We just need someone to help out."

Mrs. Coates laughed. "I could be the team mother. That's what I'm good at," she said. "Don't you agree, Thurlow? Don't you think that would be nice?"

Thurlow didn't say a word, but a look of defeat was in his eyes. And Robbie had new hope. He had an eleventh player—and an assistant coach.

When he got home, he made the crucial call, and he got more good news. Cindy Jones, Gloria's and Tracy's friend, had agreed to play. Number twelve. Now all Robbie had to do was substitute Cindy for Tony, and the team was alive.

So Robbie got on the phone. He called Coach Carlton and told him the good news. "I think my cousin isn't coming after all," he said. "But we found a girl to take his place, and Thurlow is playing for sure now. I also got us an assistant coach."

"Well, fine," the coach said. "But I don't know what's up down at the rec office. They're saying we didn't qualify after all. I guess they called your mother about this cousin of yours, and your mom said she never heard of such a person."

"Oh."

About then Robbie's mom walked into his room. From the look on her face, Robbie knew that Thurlow wasn't the only kid who was in trouble with his mother.

CHAPTER SIX

Robbie admitted everything to his mother and then to his father. They didn't yell at him, but Robbie almost wished they had. What he felt was their disappointment in him, and that was worse.

The following morning, after a miserable night, Robbie and his parents drove to the Recreation Department, where they met with Mr. Ahern, the league president. He sat behind a desk across from Robbie and his parents, who were both off from work, since it was Saturday. Coach Carlton was there, too, instead of at the morning practice, sitting next to Robbie.

Mr. Ahern seemed like a nice man. He wasn't all dressed up in a suit and tie, and he didn't start by chewing Robbie out. Rather, he leaned back in his chair and said, "Robbie, I'd just like you to explain to me how all this happened."

"You mean about saying I had a cousin named Tony when I really don't?"

Mr. Ahern smiled just a little and said, "Yes."

"Some of us turned in our applications late, and—"

"I know about that part."

"Okay. Well, we hunted all over for twelve players, and we only found eleven. We were down to the last few minutes, and I got the idea of making someone up."

"Why didn't you come inside and tell Mrs. Barker what your situation was?"

"She said we had to have twelve players by two o'clock. If we didn't, none of us could play."

"So you wanted to play so bad you were willing to lie?"

Robbie looked at the floor. He was tired of stomachaches and worries, but this was the first time anyone had actually put into words what he had done.

"What he told me last night," Mrs. Marquez said, "was that he only wanted to delay the deadline another day or two so they could find more players. He knew he was telling a lie, but he thought it wouldn't hurt anything."

Mr. Ahern didn't respond to that immediately, and for a long time the room was silent. Mr. Ahern finally asked, "Robbie, have you ever stopped to think why a city bothers to offer sports leagues for kids?"

Robbie shrugged. "It's good exercise, I guess," he said.

Mr. Ahern was sitting with his muscular arms folded over his broad chest. He looked as though he had probably played sports himself. "That's certainly part of it," he said, "but we also aim to teach you sportsmanship, teamwork, confidence—a lot of things. The only thing is, sometimes I wonder whether sports haven't started to teach just the opposite. All the news these days is about the superstars in sports, not about teamwork. And I see a lot of professional athletes setting a terrible example for the kids who look up to them."

Robbie had heard his dad say things like that, and he thought he understood. What he couldn't figure out was why Mr. Ahern wanted to talk about all that right now.

"Here's the problem I see," Mr. Ahern said.

"Kids who are good athletes sometimes get away with things they shouldn't. A high school boy lets his grades slip, but the coach wants to win, so he stretches a rule, talks to a teacher—and they make it all right for the boy to play. Why? Because that coach and everyone connected to the school, including all the parents, want to win. What we're getting is a win-at-any-cost attitude—even if we have to lie or cheat just a little."

Now Robbie saw the connection.

"The last thing I want to teach you, Robbie, is that if you love baseball, it's okay to do anything so you can play. Do you understand that?"

Robbie nodded. "I'm sorry I did it," he said. "I've been having stomachaches."

"Well, I'll say this," Mr. Ahern said, "I'm glad that lying gave you stomachaches. I'm afraid that too many people are able to lie without difficulty. Your parents must have taught you the right things."

Robbie hated to see how upset his parents looked. "They have taught me the right things," he said. "But could I ask you one thing?"

"Sure."

"I was wondering if maybe the team could still find some other players, and maybe I would be the only one kicked out of the league—since I'm the one who lied."

"Is that what you consider the fair solution to this whole problem?"

"Maybe."

Robbie was sad. It was all gone. Batting third. Playing shortstop. And having such a great coach.

"Robbie, let me ask you something," Mr. Ahern said. "Do you think we handled things right? Did the league and the recreation office do things the way we should have?"

"I guess so," Robbie said.

"Well, I'm not so sure. I've had some parents tell me we didn't advertise the deadline well enough, and that's why we had so many late applicants."

"We knew the deadline. We just messed up getting our papers in."

"Still, once Mrs. Barker decided to let you organize another team, I don't think it was fair to give you just those few hours to find twelve players."

"We had six to start with. And she had to have the schedule out by the next day."

"I know. But here's what I'm up against. On the one hand, I don't want you to get away with lying. But on the other hand, I hate to see a boy who worked so hard to get a team together miss a whole season." He looked at Mr. and Mrs. Marquez. "How do you feel about that?"

"I don't want him to get off easy," Robbie's dad said.

"But I do think he's learned his lesson," his mom added. "He's not just faking it."

"What do you think, Coach?" Mr. Ahern asked.

"Well . . . I look at this from a little different angle. When I coach, I like to win as much as the next guy. But I'm a lot more interested in teaching the game and teaching kids to play together. You know one thing about this boy—that he did something wrong. But I see him out on that field, giving everything he's got. And he's not one of those hotheaded kids who's yelling at his teammates. He thinks of his team first."

Mrs. Marquez said, "He told me last night, and I believe him, that he was going to turn himself in several days ago, but he didn't want to get the whole team disqualified and let all the other kids down."

Mr. Ahern nodded. He was still sitting with his arms folded, but now he was thinking things over. "The first problem," he said, "is that we have to have twelve players on a team. Part of the reason for that is the safety of the kids. We don't want a kid with a sore arm or ankle out there playing because there aren't enough subs."

"We found one more player last night," Robbie said.

"So you have twelve?"

"Only if you count me."

Mr. Ahern was thinking again, and Robbie's breath was caught somewhere deep in his chest. "All right. Here's what we'll do. Robbie, I want you to go to your teammates, tell them what you did and how the whole team could have been at risk, and apologize. Then I want you to do some community service. We can use a lot of help around this office. There's yard work outside, sweeping and cleaning inside. How do you feel about that as a punishment?"

"I'd like to do that." Robbie couldn't believe what he was feeling. He was coming back to life.

"I don't think you'll find it all that fun after a few days. Talk to Mrs. Barker, and she'll work out a schedule for you."

Robbie was nodding.

"I still need to talk to the other boys who were involved in this."

"It was all my idea," Robbie said.

"Maybe so. But they need to pay a price as well." He stood up. "Well, I'm relieved," he said, and he laughed. "I didn't know how I was going to tell Jack Gibbs that he bought a bunch of uniforms that we weren't going to use."

"You mean we have our uniforms now?" Robbie asked.

"Yep," the coach said. "Mr. Gibbs dropped off the uniforms early this morning." The coach chuckled. "They're ugly—the shirts and caps are sort of rust colored, like scrap iron—but I kind of like them." Then he said, "Wanda Coates is over at the park with the team. We better get over there right away ourselves. We need to get busy now that we have a team for sure."

"I've got to go home and change my clothes and get my glove," Robbie said. "Then I'll be right over."

Robbie felt like running, not walking, as he headed out the door. It was as though his body were full of helium. Outside, his dad told his mom, "Let me run Robbie back to the house so you can get going." His parents had driven over in separate cars since his mother had several errands to run. Robbie looked up at his dad as the two headed for his pickup truck.

Suddenly, the helium escaped. Robbie could still see the disappointment in his father's eyes.

They reached the truck, but when they got inside Mr. Marquez took hold of the steering wheel and looked straight ahead. He didn't start the engine. "Let me tell you something about concrete, Robbie," he said.

"What?"

"When I have to pour a lot of concrete—like when I'm pouring a basement floor—it's easier to work with the stuff when it has a lot of water in it. It flows better. But if I pour concrete that's too wet, it doesn't hold up nearly as long. It will start to chip and crack after a few years. In a basement, that can be a real problem for the owners."

Robbie nodded, but he had no idea what this was all about.

"Some cement contractors tell the delivery guy to add a lot of water to the mix—that makes the work easier. And once they finish the job, the floor looks fine. So they walk away and the customer is happy. It's only years later that the customer finds out that he didn't get what he paid for. Do you understand what I'm telling you?"

"I guess so."

"Robbie, when I pour that concrete, I have to know within myself that I've done the right thing. Maybe you think you didn't hurt anyone by telling a few lies. But the league has rules—for good reason—and you made it look like you were doing what you were supposed to do. But you weren't playing it straight with people. That's wrong. You have to feel that inside yourself."

"I did, Dad. And I didn't like it."

"Okay. Just don't forget the way you felt." Then he drove Robbie home.

While Robbie was changing his clothes and riding his bike to the park, he thought about the pride he had in his father, who did things the right way. But he also thought about the boy the coach had talked about—the one who cared so much about the team. He wanted to be more like that, for real.

Those were the things on Robbie's mind when he stood in front of the team and apologized. He told the whole story, but he had the feeling that most of the players didn't think it was that big of a deal. Gloria even told him afterward, "Hey, this worked out okay. If you ask me, you did the smart thing."

Robbie looked at her for a time, and then he said, "If I ever build a house, I don't want you to pour the concrete in my basement."

"What?"

But Robbie let it go. There were some lessons people had to learn for themselves.

The Scrappers had a pretty good practice that day. The only complaining was about the ugly uniforms. Gloria admitted that her dad had got them cheap by buying a color no one else wanted, but when the complaints got a little too harsh for her ears, she told everyone to shut up and stop whining. They were lucky to have a sponsor at all. And no one could deny that.

Thurlow also got a lot of attention. He seemed to take no interest in being there, but during batting practice, he hit some killer drives. He ran pretty well in the outfield, too, but Robbie could tell that he was capable of running much faster if he wanted to. When the coach asked him what position he wanted to play, he merely shrugged.

Wanda Coates said, "He can play anything. He's not showing what he can do today."

Coach Carlton nodded. "Well, we may give you a chance to play a little right field," he said.

But he got no rise out of Thurlow, who shrugged again.

Wanda, who had told the kids not to call her Mrs. Coates, turned out to be a great addition to the team. She was all over the field, cheering and encouraging, and she knew more about baseball than she had let on. Everyone liked her, too, including the coach.

So Robbie felt pretty good as he headed home from practice. He finally had a team—even if it was a pretty strange collection of kids. And the lying was over.

CHAPTER SEVEN

The Scrappers practiced every day that week. And Coach Carlton was amazing. He never seemed as old as he was. No matter how hot it got, or how long the practice lasted, he seemed to have as much energy as the kids. He was always teaching, too. Guys like Chad and Martin, who had never been interested in sports—and were lousy players—got as much attention as anyone. The coach was constantly showing them how to get down on a ground ball or how to position their feet for a strong throw; and no question about it, they were getting better. The new girl, Cindy Jones, wasn't as good as Gloria or Tracy, but she had all the fundamentals right, and she didn't make a lot of dumb mistakes.

By the time the next game came around on

Friday night, Robbie was beginning to believe that the team could make a decent showing. He didn't expect to win. After all, the game was against the Mustangs, a team everyone said was probably the best in the league. Still, the Scrappers had some pretty good players, and the coach had them doing a lot of things right.

On Friday evening Robbie got to the park early and warmed up with his friends. Almost everyone seemed psyched and ready to play.

But then Robbie started noticing the kids who played for the Mustangs. They had cool uniforms: white pants with black shirts and hats. They looked confident, too, like guys who had played a lot of baseball in their lives.

The Scrappers looked sort of silly by comparison. The word *Scrappers* was printed in large letters on the front of their shirts. On the backs, *Jack's Scrap and Salvage* and a number appeared.

Before the game started, Coach Carlton called the kids together. He read off the lineup, and most of the positions had stayed the same. But Robbie was stunned. He was playing third base and Gloria was at shortstop.

Trent, who was sitting next to Robbie on the

grass, whispered, "He's just giving her a try at it—you know, to be fair."

Robbie nodded. He thought that was probably right. He told himself he had to play hard at third and do his best for the team. But then he saw Tracy slap hands with Gloria, heard both of them laugh, and suddenly he felt rotten. He knew what the coach had said about his being a team player, but he still wanted to be the shortstop.

"How come Thurlow isn't in the lineup?" Trent whispered.

Robbie had been thinking so much about his own change that he hadn't noticed. All week everyone had been talking about how good Thurlow was, and what a difference he would make—and now the coach had him sitting on the bench. But Robbie thought he understood why. "Thurlow doesn't try," he said. "And the coach hates that. Martin didn't care much about playing at first, but he's doing his best now."

"I just hope the coach puts Thurlow in before long," Trent said. "Maybe Martin tries hard, but he drops almost every ball that comes to him."

Robbie had to admit that was true, and Chad was even worse. Cindy was better than either one of them, but the coach was using her to sub in the infield. "What we've got to hope for," Robbie said, "is that Adam can throw some strikes tonight. If he keeps walking guys, it doesn't matter what else happens."

"I think Ollie's a better pitcher," Trent said.

"I know. In practice. But last year, when he got into games, he would get too nervous, and then he would walk everybody, just like Adam."

It wasn't a pretty picture, overall, but both Adam and Ollie were tall guys with long arms, and Ollie especially could really hum the ball when he got in a groove. Both guys might do all right if they could learn to calm down.

The Scrappers were up first, so Robbie walked over and looked for the bat he had liked best at practice. He was giving it a swing when the coach walked over to him. "Robbie," he said, "I hope you're not too disappointed, but I've decided I want to have you play third all the time now. Plan on practicing at that position, and work hard on the long throw you have to make."

"Okay," Robbie tried to say, but hardly anything came out.

The coach obviously sensed his disappointment. "The thing is, Gloria has a little more range than you do. She's quicker, I think, so she does a little better at getting to balls hit deep in the hole or covering second on a double play. I thought about putting her at third because her arm is a little stronger than yours, but I think that's something you can work on. If you work hard, you can be a first-rate third baseman."

Robbie had been feeling bad before, but now he felt like a swimmer going down in a whirlpool. She was quicker? Covered more ground? Had a stronger arm? What was left? Maybe the coach liked the size of her mouth better, too.

Robbie walked into the dugout and sat down. By the time he got there, he had gone from disappointment to anger. Maybe old Coach Carlton didn't know so much after all. Robbie knew he was as quick as Gloria, any day, and his throw from third wasn't always that great, but neither was hers.

Adam sat down next to him and gave him a

nudge with his elbow. "I can't believe you let a girl beat you out," he said, and he laughed.

"Just shut up, okay?" Robbie snapped. "Try to throw a strike once in a while, or Gloria will have to replace *you*."

Adam stood up. He had his usual "Where am I anyway?" look on his face. "Hey," he said, "I was just kidding." He walked to the end of the dugout and sat down next to Ollie, and then the two began to talk.

This isn't over yet, Robbie told himself. *We'll see who can cover ground out there tonight.*

When Gloria walked into the dugout, she said, in a voice that could break bricks, "All right. Let's get some hits. Let's beat these guys!"

Robbie knew what that was all about. Now that she had what she wanted, she was going to start acting like she was the big shot on the team. Team captain or something.

Jeremy walked out to the batter's box, and the Scrappers all stood at the fence and yelled for him to get a hit. But Robbie stayed in his seat. Or at least he did until he glanced toward the other end of the bench and saw Thurlow, the only other player sitting down. Suddenly he didn't feel right. So he stood up and tried to yell for Jeremy. He just couldn't get much heart into it.

Jeremy was too anxious, as usual, and he swung at two terrible pitches. But then he calmed down and let a couple go by for balls. He fouled one off after that. Then, taking a signal from Coach Carlton, he squared away and laid down a two-strike bunt. It wasn't perfect, but the third baseman was taken by surprise. By the time he got to the ball and made the throw, Jeremy had crossed first base.

Tracy was batting second today. She played it smart, didn't swing at anything bad, and walked on five pitches.

Robbie marched to the plate with all kinds of thoughts running through his head. He wanted to crush one and show the coach he had some power. But he needed to prove he knew the game. This was a time to hit behind the runners and move them into scoring position. He thought of players like Bobby Richardson, in the old days, or his greatest hero, Alex Rodriguez. They knew how to move base runners.

He stepped into the box and took his stance,

but he felt tight, nervous. The pitch came down the middle, and Robbie watched it all the way. But for some reason, he didn't trigger.

"Strike one!"

Swing, stupid, he told himself.

And he did swing at the next pitch, even though it was clearly outside. Now there were two strikes on him.

Robbie stepped out of the box to collect himself. As he took a practice swing and tried to clear his head, he heard his father yell, "You can do it, buddy. Just hang in there."

But that didn't help. It only reminded him that his parents were expecting big things from him.

Robbie took a deep breath and stepped back to the plate. But the pitcher threw a change-up, and Robbie was too eager. He swung way too soon.

And struck out.

The Mustangs worked him over as he walked back to the dugout, but he tried not to listen. He tossed his bat away and then met Gloria, who was coming out to the on-deck circle. "Don't worry about it, Robbie," she said.

But that only made him angrier. He knew what she was really thinking.

Robbie sat down on the bench. About then the sound of a bat drew his attention back to the field. Wilson had just hit a hard shot to left field. Jeremy rounded third and came home to score. Tracy stopped at second.

Now Gloria stepped into the box. Robbie couldn't believe how cocky she acted. She was wearing wristbands and batting gloves, and she went through the whole routine—knocking dirt from her shoes and all the rest—like she thought she was a major leaguer.

She took the first pitch, and then she went through the whole act again. But the next pitch was belt high, and she took a smooth, level swing. The ball shot off her bat and darted toward the gap in left center. It bounced between the outfielders and rolled to the fence. Two runs scored. Gloria only stopped at second because the coach held up his arms and yelled for her not to try for third.

And then she had to show off some more. She waved her clenched fist at the bench and yelled, "All right, everybody hits. Let's keep it going."

One more shot at Robbie.

When Trent rolled a little grounder back to the pitcher, Robbie was sort of relieved. At least he wasn't the only one who had made an out. But when Adam popped the ball up for the third out, the rally was suddenly over. Still, the Scrappers had picked up three runs. They were off to a good start.

As Robbie trotted out to third base, he told himself to forget his strikeout, settle down, and have himself a great game in the field.

And he got his chance almost immediately. The first batter slashed one up the third base line. Robbie reacted quickly, fielded the ball cleanly on the first hop, set his feet, and threw to first. Ollie had to stretch a little high for it, but he made the grab.

All Robbie's teammates shouted to him, told him he had made a good play, and Robbie felt a lot better.

"Nice job," Gloria said.

Robbie nodded to her.

But she just couldn't resist. "Of course, I would have made a better throw." She laughed.

Robbie turned away. He wasn't going to let this girl bother him.

The next batter punched the ball to the left side. Robbie broke left. It was a ball the third baseman was supposed to take, if he could reach it, but he just couldn't get there. Gloria had cut to her right, though. She backhanded the ball, put on the brakes, then turned and fired. It was a "bang, bang" play, but the ump called the runner safe.

Still, it was an amazing stop and a perfect throw. Robbie had to wonder whether he could have done as well. "Wow. Great play," he told Gloria, and he meant it.

"I should have had him," Gloria said, and she took an angry kick at the dirt. The girl had dirt all over her already, somehow, even though the game had just started.

Robbie was thinking that Gloria really was better than he was, and that idea was more than he wanted to face. He told himself, in self-defense, that he was going to practice harder than he ever had before, spend the whole summer making himself a better fielder.

The next batter hit a high fly to right. It should have been an easy out. Martin ran in for the ball, got under it, but it hit the heel of his glove and popped out. Then the big kid who played first base—Alan Pingree—pounded a line drive between Trent and Jeremy. It fell in for a double and two runs scored.

Adam seemed to let that get to him. He walked the next batter, and then, for a while, nothing went right. When the Scrappers finally got out of the inning, the Mustangs were ahead 7 to 3. The worst part was, Robbie had made a bad throw to first that had allowed one of the runs to score.

Robbie only had one good memory from the whole mess: Gloria had booted an easy grounder. She had thrown a fit about that, and the coach had yelled to her to stay down on the ball, to not try to throw before she had it. Robbie had loved every second of it.

He knew very well he wasn't supposed to do that. He couldn't help thinking about the things the coach had said about him. But losing his position to *Gloria* was simply more than he could take.

In the second inning, Robbie came up to bat again. This time Tracy was on first with two away. He waited for a good pitch, and then he whacked a clean single up the middle. As it turned out, Wilson struck out, and the Scrappers scored no runs in the inning. So the score was still 7 to 3. But at least Robbie finally had his first hit of the season. And that was something to feel good about. He had something to prove tonight.

CHAPTER EIGHT

Over the next three innings Adam settled down. He didn't overpower anyone, and he still walked some batters; but the Scrappers played decent defense, and the Mustangs only got one run in the second inning and none in the third and fourth. The only trouble was, the Scrappers couldn't get anything going at all, so the score was 8 to 3 when they came up in the fifth.

Jeremy led off. He rolled an easy grounder to second base, but the second baseman tried to hurry his throw and bounced it in the dirt. The first baseman couldn't dig it out, and Jeremy was safe.

Tracy also got lucky. She slapped a little shot into left, and the shortstop ran back for it. But he turned the wrong way. By the time he twisted back around, the ball dropped in.

The Mustangs seemed to be opening the door, and Robbie came up to bat wanting to be the guy to come through in the pinch. This time he wanted to be an RBI man: Ken Griffey Jr. or Mo Vaughn.

"Make him pitch to you," the coach yelled. Robbie looked toward the third base coach's box and nodded. Then he laid off the first two pitches, both balls. With the count at 2 and 0, he knew the pitcher would try to get the ball over the plate.

Easy, easy, relax, he told himself. *Don't swing too hard. Just meet the ball.*

He saw the ball all the way, and he took a good swing. He connected solidly and drove the ball to the right side. The first baseman lunged at the ball, but it slipped under his glove and bounced on down the right field line.

Robbie saw Wanda waving her arm for him to keep going, so he rolled around first and charged on to second. Jeremy and Tracy scored ahead of him. The score was now 8 to 5, and there were still no outs. Maybe the Scrappers weren't out of this game after all. And maybe Robbie could end up the RBI leader for the year.

But Wilson struck out. When Gloria came up, Robbie hardly knew what to think. Deep down, he hoped that she would strike out and that someone else could drive him in.

Gloria didn't strike out, but she lifted a lazy fly into left, and the left fielder jogged in and caught it. Then Trent knocked a grounder straight to the first baseman, and the inning was over.

Robbie ran back to the dugout to get his glove. Just as he got there, Trent caught up with him. "You're doing better than she is," Trent said. "Now I hope she makes some more errors."

Robbie nodded, but as he trotted back onto the field, he felt strange. Trent ought to be hoping for the team to win, not wishing the worst on Gloria. Robbie knew what he had been thinking himself, but it sounded worse when he heard someone say it out loud.

And then the words came back to him. "He thinks of his team first," the coach had said.

"All right, let's mow 'em down," Robbie yelled. He looked over at Gloria. "We can still win this game," he told her.

And she said, "That's right. Let's throw some leather at them."

But Adam didn't get off to a good start. He walked the first batter on a 3 and 2 count, and then he seemed to fall apart. He walked the next guy without ever coming close to the strike zone. That's when Coach Carlton walked to the mound. He waved for Ollie to come over. Robbie and Gloria also walked to the mound.

"Are you getting tired?" the coach asked Adam.

"I don't know," Adam said. And he seemed completely serious when he said, "Sometimes I think the plate moves. I guess it doesn't really, but . . ."

"Well, take a rest. Go sit down. I'm going to have Ollie pitch. Tell Cindy to come out and play first base."

Robbie couldn't believe it. Chad was now playing in right field for Martin. Thurlow was the only guy who hadn't played. He was still sitting at the end of the bench, with his arms crossed, hardly paying any attention to the game. But he had to be better at first base than Cindy. She was a pretty good fielder, but she was short, and Robbie didn't think she had ever played the position.

Adam handed the ball to the coach and walked back to the dugout.

"Here you go," Coach Carlton said, and he handed the ball to Ollie. "Don't think too much. Just throw strikes. The defense will back you up."

Ollie nodded, but Robbie knew the guy's mind was moving fast. And so were his lips. He hardly seemed to know that he was talking to himself.

Ollie could actually throw the ball a little harder than Adam, but his control was just as shaky. Putting him on the mound was a lot like putting green wood on a fire: you knew you'd get a lot of smoke, but there was no telling where it would go. Robbie hated to think what might happen.

And sure enough, Ollie was all over the place with the ball. Cindy missed a couple of throws that Adam probably would have handled. Chad misjudged a fly ball, and that cost the team another run. But just when the game seemed to be turning into a complete rout, Tracy made a good play to snag a line drive, and then Gloria fielded a ground ball and ran to second for a force out that ended the inning. The Mustangs had pushed across four runs, though, and the score was now 12 to 5.

When the Scrappers walked to the dugout, the coach was the only one still trying to talk it up. "Come on, kids, keep your heads up," he called. "Let's get a rally going and get back into this thing."

But the players gathered in the dugout in little groups. The three girls sat together, and Robbie heard Gloria say, "If we had a decent pitcher, we might have a chance."

Ollie was leading off, so he was outside the dugout, but there was no way he could have missed Gloria's whisper—which was loud as a hurricane.

Martin and Chad always stayed together. Robbie heard Chad say something about Gloria and her mouth.

Robbie also heard Thurlow tell Wilson that he didn't care whether he played or not.

Trent walked over to Robbie. "What'd the coach put Cindy on first for? That won't work."

Robbie, of course, had been thinking the same thing, but he didn't want to criticize the coach. The fact was, all this negative talk—and breaking off into groups—made Robbie feel strange. He was trying to think of something to say without sounding too goody-goody when the coach called, "Wait a second, ump. Time-out." He walked from his coach's box over to the dugout. "What's going on in here?" he said.

No one answered.

"Gloria, what's going on?"

"I don't know."

"I think you do. Tell me."

"Nothing. Everybody's just getting fed up with the way we're playing."

"Okay. I can understand that. But what have you been saying? Who are you blaming the problem on?"

Now Gloria was really on the spot. She answered, softly, "Ollie, I guess. And Adam." She shrugged. "You've gotta admit, our pitching has been rotten."

"Ollie, are you doing your best?" the coach asked.

"Yes. But I'm not doing very well."

"What about you, Adam? Did you walk those batters on purpose?"

"No."

"Good. Are you mad at anyone?"

"Me?"

"Yeah. Who are you blaming the problem on?"

"I don't know. It just upset me a little when Chad missed that fly. I finally made a good pitch, and then—"

"Chad, are you doing your best?"

"Yeah."

"You wanted to catch that fly, didn't you?"

"Sure I did."

"I believe it. But who are you mad at?"

"Gloria," he answered, without hesitation. "She doesn't have any right to yell at me."

"Well, it seems like we've come full circle, doesn't it?" Coach Carlton shook his head and chuckled. "I'll tell you what. I think we're going to get beat today. Anybody agree?"

Robbie had never heard a coach say anything like that, and from the looks on the others' faces, Robbie guessed they hadn't either.

"With the talent we have, I suppose we might

have a chance to come back and win," the coach said. "But you kids aren't a team. You're all mad at one another. Nothing very good is going to happen that way. I can tell you that right now."

No one said a word.

"I don't like to lose, but I can live with it. Every team is going to lose sometimes. But all you kids getting mad at one another—I can't take that. It ruins everything. There's no fun in the game when you act like that."

"Come on, Coach. Let's have a batter," the umpire yelled.

"All right. Just a second," the coach called back. A lot of shamefaced players were looking at the ground by this time. "Anybody here had a perfect game today?" Coach Carlton asked.

He waited, but no one answered.

"No? So I guess there's nobody here who's got much to say about anybody else. How about you all start pulling for one another, backing one another up? How about acting like a team?"

The umpire was calling for a batter again. "All right. We're coming," the coach shouted. Then he said, "Wilson, do you have anything you want to say?"

Robbie could see Wilson's shock at being called on. But he stood up, still wearing his shin guards. "The coach is right," he said. "If we're going to lose, let's at least lose together."

Wanda said, "That's exactly right, Wilson. But let's *win* together. We can still do it."

"All right then," Coach Carlton said. "Let's play some ball—and forget all the rest. Go out there, Ollie, and do your best."

"Yeah!" Robbie yelled. "Come on, Ollie!" And everyone picked up the chant.

Ollie wasn't much of a hitter, though, and he only managed to hit a little bouncer back to the mound. The pitcher threw him out. Robbie was afraid that would shut down all the new enthusiasm. But the cheering continued, even though it was Chad coming up. Robbie sort of expected the coach to put Thurlow in at that point, but it didn't happen, and Robbie told himself not to second-guess the coach.

But Chad struck out.

Still, the Scrappers talked it up. "Come on, Jeremy, we can win this game!" Wilson bellowed.

The Mustang players seemed to think that

was funny, and even some of the people in the bleachers laughed, but Jeremy poked the first pitch down the line in left and zipped around to second for a double. Then Tracy knocked the ball on the ground to the right side, and the ball slipped through for a single. Jeremy scored.

Robbie had to keep it going. He didn't get the hit he wanted, but he fouled off a couple, kept waiting, and finally worked the pitcher for a walk.

As Wilson walked to the plate, Robbie called out, "Park one over the fence, Wilson!"

"All right. I think I will," he yelled back, and a lot of people in the crowd laughed.

Wilson stepped to the plate, all hunched over, looking more like a grizzly bear than a baseball player. And then he took an awkward, hard swing at the first pitch—and almost fell down.

Once again, people were laughing.

But they didn't laugh when he caught the next pitch flush. He hit a screamer that jumped out of the park so fast that the left fielder hardly had time to move. Suddenly the Scrappers didn't look so foolish for thinking they could still win. The score was 12 to 9, and Gloria was walking confidently to the plate.

She hit the ball hard, too, but she smacked it straight at the shortstop, who snagged it for the out.

Robbie yelled, "Nice swat. You were robbed." He grabbed his glove and headed for third base. "Let's shut them down. We've got one more chance," he yelled.

All the players were talking it up now, and Ollie was talking to himself—and looking determined. But maybe he tried too hard. Once again, he walked the first batter.

Robbie glanced over at Gloria. He hoped she wouldn't start complaining, but she yelled, "Get this next guy, Ollie. You're okay."

Ollie glanced at her for just a moment, just enough to show he had heard. But the support seemed to please him.

"The play's at second," Tracy shouted. "Come on, Ollie."

Ollie made a pretty good pitch, but the batter smacked it hard up the middle.

Gloria and Tracy both broke for the ball. Gloria had a better shot at it, so Tracy was smart enough to veer off and back her up.

Gloria was moving at full speed when she stretched out and short-hopped the ball. She took a couple more steps, got her balance, stepped on second, and then fired a perfect throw to Cindy.

Cindy looked wide-eyed at the speed of Gloria's throw, but she made the catch for the double play.

Robbie found himself running toward Gloria. He clapped her on the back, and she turned around. "*Great* play!" he said.

"Thanks," she said, and shrugged. Her jaw had never stopped working a big chunk of gum in her cheek.

Over the other noise from the crowd a booming voice shouted, "That's my *Scrapper*!"

Jack Gibbs. There was no mistaking the voice. It was even louder than Gloria's.

Gloria ducked her head for a moment, but when she looked up, she was laughing.

"Hey, he's right," Robbie said. "I gotta tell you—I don't think I could have made that play."

"Yeah, but you do all right for a boy."

Robbie and Gloria both laughed.

The next batter fouled off a couple of pitches. Then he took a big swing and sent an accidental bunt rolling toward third.

Robbie charged the ball and picked it up with his bare hand while still on the run. In one smooth motion, without ever straightening up, he fired underhand to first.

The throw was a gunshot, and right on target. It almost knocked Cindy over, but she made the catch.

"Yer *out*!" the ump barked.

The crowd cheered, and Robbie leaped into the air. And then Gloria was there, slapping him on the back, screaming into his ear, "Hey, I couldn't have made that one!"

CHAPTER NINE

The enthusiasm that brought the Scrappers off the field carried over easily into their time at bat. They lined the dugout and cheered for one another. Thurlow was the only one staying out of the excitement. The players all knew this was the last chance to catch the Mustangs. They needed three runs to tie.

Trent was up first and the bottom of the order followed. Robbie knew that the chances of scoring three runs with Cindy, Ollie, and possibly Chad coming up were not good. But the momentum had swung to the Scrappers. Who knew what might happen? The Mustangs' chatter sounded sort of cranky. "Come on, we can't let these guys back in the game," they were yelling, and now they seemed to be the ones blaming one another.

"Don't walk anybody, Derek," Pingree was yelling from first base.

"Let's go, Trent! Get it going!" Tracy yelled. And she sounded like she really expected him to do it.

In the bleachers, people were yelling for both sides. Robbie loved the whole scene. This was why he loved baseball.

He also had the feeling that the Mustangs' pitcher was getting tired. Derek Salinas was his name, and he was good, but he had thrown a lot of pitches tonight. His fastball wasn't popping the way it had early in the game.

Trent had a quiet way of going about his business. He worked the pitcher to a 3 and 1 count, got his pitch, and then yanked it past the third baseman. He rounded first and bluffed a move to second, but the left fielder had gotten to the ball quickly, so Wanda shouted to him to hold up, and he did.

Cindy was batting for the first time. Robbie didn't know what to expect from her. She didn't look nervous, and when she took the first two pitches, Robbie thought she was playing it smart. But when she took another pitch down the middle for a strike, he knew she didn't want to swing. She was hoping for a walk.

Salinas clearly sensed that, too, and he tossed another one straight down the middle. Cindy didn't even move her bat. The count moved to 2 and 2.

"Come on, Cindy. You have to trigger on those good ones," the coach was yelling. He clapped his hands.

But the next pitch was in the strike zone again, and Cindy swung way too hard. She missed the ball by a mile. The catcher did drop the ball, but he picked it up quickly and tagged her before she could take off.

Now the noise was coming from the field and from the Mustangs' dugout. Robbie felt some of the air go out of his teammates. But Ollie was walking to the plate, and he was talking to himself. Robbie knew he was telling himself that he could get a hit.

But the pitcher was obviously confident again. He fired a good fastball, and Ollie missed it clean.

Robbie was starting to face reality. The wrong players were coming up to bat. The

Scrappers were scrappy, maybe, but some of them just weren't very good hitters.

Ollie swung again at the next pitch, and this time he topped the ball and hit a high chopper toward the shortstop. A fast runner might have had a chance, but Ollie seemed to take forever to get his long legs going. The shortstop charged the ball, took it on a high hop, and . . . threw it over the head of the first baseman!

Ollie was on, and suddenly the Scrappers, about to be buried, were still alive.

All the players in the dugout were going wild. Robbie hadn't noticed that Coach Carlton had walked to the dugout. "Thurlow," he said, "I want you to bat for Chad."

Robbie had forgotten all about Thurlow, who was still sitting in the corner of the dugout. Everyone was supposed to play, and this was one of the last chances.

Thurlow looked at the coach with disgust, obviously mad that he had been left to sit so long. But he got up and slowly walked from the dugout. He picked up a bat without paying any attention to its weight, and he walked to the batter's box. The Scrappers were all yelling for him to lose one over the fence, but he stepped to the plate and just stood there. He didn't seem ready, didn't even seem to care.

"Come on, Thurlow," Robbie yelled. "You can do it." And, of course, Robbie was thinking that three runs would tie the game. But it wouldn't happen if Thurlow didn't make an effort.

"Thurlow," Wanda shouted, "you get serious. You do this."

But he continued to stand with his bat low, his legs straight. Robbie wondered if he might strike out on purpose, just to spite his mother.

But the first pitch was over the plate, and Thurlow suddenly snapped into action. He lashed at the ball and got all of it. It soared high and long, and it had the distance to clear the fence. Robbie spun toward left field, his breath caught in his chest. But the ball was bending foul.

Strike one.

Thurlow had trotted a few steps toward first. Now he came back, picked up his bat, and stood at the plate again. But once again, he seemed not to be ready. He let a pitch sail by for a ball. And then another.

But the next pitch was in there, and again he jumped on it. And again he got around on it and pulled it long and foul. It would have been a homer had it been fair, though, and all Robbie could think was that, somehow, he had to hit one like that in fair territory.

Thurlow took another pitch, and the count was full. Something had to give.

The pitcher took the sign, then took a deep breath. He checked the runners, who were both leading off, waiting, watching. Robbie's breath held tight.

The pitch was good, and Thurlow sprung to life again. He jacked the ball high and long toward left field. This one was clearly fair—and long. It sailed toward the fence in left center, and both the left fielder and the center fielder ran all out to try to get to it.

Everything was silent. The ball kept arching toward the fence, and the fielders kept running. Then both reached up, as they pinched toward each other.

The ball was coming down, down . . .

"Go over, go over. . . ," Robbie heard himself whispering.

But it didn't make it. The ball dropped beyond the reach of the outfielders just inside the fence and bounced over the wall.

It was a ground-rule double.

For a moment Robbie felt nothing but disappointment. Then he realized that the Scrappers hadn't tied the game, but they were nevertheless in good shape. A run had scored, and runners were now on second and third with the top of the order coming up.

Jeremy approached the batter's box, and Tracy walked out to the on-deck circle. Suddenly Robbie realized that he might be the guy standing at the plate with the game on the line. That scared him a little, but he still liked the idea.

Jeremy didn't waste any time. He went after the first pitch, as usual, and he did the smart thing. He tried to punch a hit to the right side, tried to bring those two runs home. But the ball bounced right to the second baseman.

A run scored, but the second baseman threw Jeremy out at first. So now there were two outs, and the Scrappers were down by one. But Thurlow was the fastest guy in the park, and all Tracy had to do was stay alive. If she could score Thurlow, Robbie would come up with a chance to drive in the go-ahead run.

The crowd in the park was going crazy. And the only person making more noise than Gloria was her dad. "Knock that ball out of here, Tracy!" he shouted, and it sounded almost like a threat.

Robbie took some warm-up swings, and then he knelt down in the on-deck circle.

Tracy stepped to the plate. Robbie watched Salinas. He was taking long breaths, trying to stay calm. His team was telling him to blow the ball by "this girl," but Salinas had to be remembering that Tracy had poked a nice little shot to left field last time up.

Maybe Salinas wanted to scare Tracy. He pumped a smoking fastball inside and high. Tracy spun away, and then she shouted, "Hey, what was that, your change-up? Let's see your fastball."

Coach Carlton yelled, "Never mind that stuff. Just look for something you can hit."

Tracy stepped up to the plate and pawed at the ground. She was ready for whatever the pitcher had.

But now he did come with his change-up.
Tracy started to swing and then tried to hold up.
But she sent a little roller out in front of the
plate.

Tracy took off hard, digging for first, and for a
moment Robbie thought that she might have hit
the perfect bunt, by accident. Thurlow was
flashing toward the plate. But the catcher
jumped out, grabbed the ball, set himself, and
threw a strike to first base.

Suddenly the game was over.

The Scrappers had lost by one run.

Robbie was standing with a bat in his hands
and not one thing he could do with it. He took a
hard swing at the ground. The Scrappers had
come so close. He couldn't believe it had ended
so abruptly. He lifted his bat and slammed it
hard into the dirt again, but just as he did, Coach
Carlton slapped him on the back and said,
"Great game, Robbie. Don't be upset. All you
kids were terrific."

Robbie took a quick look at the scoreboard.
Was the coach confused? Did he think the
Scrappers had won? But there it was: Mustangs,
12; Scrappers, 11.

"Go shake their hands," the coach yelled. "It took a good team to beat you. You tell 'em so."

"We almost pulled it out," Robbie said.

"I know. That's what I'm so pleased about. Now you go shake hands with those guys. They're good."

So Robbie lined up with the others, and he slapped hands with all the Mustangs. "Good game. Good game," he kept mumbling, but he couldn't shake off his disappointment.

But the coach, still sounding excited, shouted, "Come over here, kids. All you parents, come over here, too."

So the players trudged over and sat down on the grass just outside the left field line, near third base. Their parents gathered around, too, with a lot of brothers and sisters.

"What a great game!" the coach said, grinning. He clapped his hands together. "Twelve to eleven—with the game on the line right up to the last out. That's what makes baseball so fun. It's the greatest game ever created."

Robbie agreed with all that. But he would have been a whole lot happier had the score been reversed.

"I don't know about all of you, but I'm getting excited about this team." Coach Carlton looked around at the parents, but he didn't get much reaction. The adults looked a little baffled, as though they thought the old fellow was losing his marbles.

It was Jack Gibbs who said, in his baritone voice, "We came pretty close anyway."

"No, that's not what I mean," the coach said. "I didn't hold out much hope of winning tonight. We started out as a bunch of kids who happened to turn in their applications late—or who got talked into playing at the last minute. They hardly know one another, and most of them have a whole lot to learn about baseball."

He hesitated and looked around as though he were surprised everyone wasn't as happy as he was. "But didn't you see what happened there in those last couple of innings? These kids started to act like a *team*."

Adam's dad said, "They came within a few inches of beating the best team in the league. I think they have a chance at the championship."

"That's right," the coach said. "I'm excited about that, too. But if they can become a real team, they'll make a memory for themselves. It'll be a summer they'll never forget, win or lose. Do you all understand that?"

Robbie wasn't sure he did. He was a lot more excited about what Adam's dad had said. But he liked the coach's enthusiasm, his love of baseball, and right now, he even liked the other players.

"Well . . . ," the coach said, and he looked down at the Scrappers, "as the year goes on, maybe you'll understand more what I'm talking about. But for right now, remember what you felt those last two innings, when everyone pulled together. That's something to build on. What do you say to a Saturday morning practice? We have a lot of stuff we need to work on."

The kids agreed to that, but when the coach was finished, Robbie saw the groups form again—the same ones he had seen earlier in the dugout. The girls got together, and so did Adam and Ollie. Chad and Martin walked away with each other, and Thurlow cleared out immediately, not even waiting for his mother. Jeremy left with his parents. He didn't seem to have a friend on the team.

Robbie and Trent and Wilson also ended up

together. "This is turning out better than I thought," Trent said. "The coach is right. We can be a good team."

"Yeah," Wilson said. "It might even be worth all those hours we've got to work down at the rec office." He laughed, and so did Trent. The three boys were going to be at the office a lot together that summer.

"The coach needs to let Thurlow play the whole game next time," Trent said. "Then we'll have a chance."

"Thurlow shouldn't play until he shows he wants to," Robbie said. "The coach isn't going to let him start until he shows the right attitude."

"Coaches always say that kind of stuff," Trent said. "But the best guys ought to be out there on the field."

"This coach means what he says," Robbie told him. "We can learn from him." Certainly, Robbie was thinking about the things he had learned.

The boys were about to leave when the three girls walked over. "Hey, you know what?" Gloria said. "You guys aren't too bad."

"Just not as good as you, right?" Trent asked.

"Of course not." She stood there with dirt all over her ugly shirt, still chewing her wad of gum. "But I'm the best. So that shouldn't make you feel too bad."

"Thurlow's the best," Wilson corrected her.

Gloria stopped chewing for a moment, and she nodded. "That's actually true," she said. "If he ever decides he wants to play, we'll have a team."

Robbie hated to admit it to himself, but he was beginning to find old Gloria almost likeable.

But then she looked at Robbie. "At least we finally got the right player at third—and a better one at shortstop."

Robbie only smiled, but what Gloria didn't know was that he was thinking she was right. Now, he just had to be the best third baseman he could possibly be. Like Wade Boggs. George Brett. Brooks Robinson. It was a great position, probably the best position of all.

TIPS FOR PLAYING THIRD BASE

1. Line up even with the bag (or a step or two behind it) for most batters. If you expect a bunt, you may want to move in closer. Play about ten feet away from the bag toward second base unless the coach tells you to make adjustments for certain batters.
2. Be alert and ready. The ball will get to you *fast* sometimes. Stay balanced, ready to move in any direction, and on the balls of your feet.
3. You need a good arm to play third because you have to make a long throw to first. But remember, an accurate throw is better than a wild one, so don't try to throw *too* hard.
4. Make sure you watch the ball into your glove and field it cleanly before you look to see where you want to throw it.
5. Once you field the ball, set your feet and get your balance. That may take a fraction of a second to do, but the speed on your throw will make up for the time you take to be ready to throw.
6. When a ball is hit between the third baseman and the shortstop, you should cut in front and field the ball if you can. Your throw is easier since you are not moving away from the other bases.
7. On a slow roller or a bunt down the third-base line, field the ball if you have a play. If you see you have no chance to make the play, let the ball roll. It may roll across the line and become a foul ball.

8. On a slow roller or a bunt, major leaguers sometimes bare-hand the ball and throw in the same motion. This can be a great play, but it takes years of practice. Sometimes you have to hang on to the ball and allow the single. That's better than a wild throw that puts the runner on second.

9. When a new batter steps to the plate, think of all the possible plays you might choose to make. How many runners are on base? How many outs? How fast are the runners? What is the score? All of these factors, and many others, may help as you choose what play to make. (Listen to your coach, who notices all of these factors.)

SOME RULES FROM COACH CARLTON

HITTING:

Keep your eyes on the ball. Both of them. Turn your head until your chin touches your shoulder. Look for the ball while it's still in the pitcher's hand and follow it all the way to your bat.

BASE RUNNING:

Run hard on every play. You may assume that you're a "dead duck," but go hard anyway. The defense just might throw the ball away. Speed also worries a fielder, and will sometimes force a mistake. Your effort also inspires all the players on your team.

BEING A TEAM PLAYER:

The only "stat" that really matters is your team's won/lost record. Don't worry about your personal numbers. If you play hard and help your team win, the numbers will take care of themselves.

ON DECK:
WILSON LOVE, CATCHER.
DON'T MISS HIS STORY IN SCRAPPERS #2: *HOME RUN HERO.*

Wilson watched the pitcher warm up. It was hard to imagine the kid could throw all that fast. He was not that tall, and he was really skinny. As Wilson stepped into the box, the catcher yelled, "All right, Bullet, fire it in here."

"Bullet?" Wilson said.

The catcher was a huge kid. He grinned as he said, "That's what we call him—Bullet Bennett."

Wilson took a deep breath. He tried to put all that out of his mind. *Don't drop your bat too low*, he told himself. *Take a level swing.*

The first pitch came like a bullet all right. And Wilson took a smooth swing. But the ball smacked into the catcher's glove before he was even halfway around.

Start your swing sooner, Wilson told himself. *But keep it smooth. Don't lash at the ball*. He took his stance—the one that felt right to him.

Another fireball! Wilson took a hard swing and—*smack!*—the ball pounded into the catcher's mitt. The big catcher grunted and then laughed. "That one stung," he chided Wilson.

Wilson told himself not to pay attention. He was mad at himself. He knew what he'd done: gone back to his old swing entirely. He had dropped his bat way down and lashed upward at the ball. So he went through his list again, told himself all the things he had to do.

The pitch was low and away. He tried to get his swing started early, then tried to stop it. His weight was thrown forward, and he stumbled, lost his balance, and fell. He ended up flat on his face, his chest across the plate.

And the ump was barking, "Steeeerrriiiike three!"

Wilson jumped up, but the damage was done. The Stingray infielders were all laughing, and someone in the crowd yelled, "Hey, kid, don't hurt yourself."

Wilson stared straight ahead as he walked to the dugout. He grabbed his catcher's gear and started to put it on, but he didn't want any of his teammates to say a word to him.

Robbie did say, "Don't worry about it, Wilson." But Wilson hardly knew how to take that. He'd never been so embarrassed in his entire life.

Wilson was bent over, near the fence, strapping on his shin guards when he heard footsteps coming toward him. He looked up to see his dad coming his way. He really didn't want this.

"Are you okay?" his father asked.

"Yeah. I'm fine."

"Look, I think maybe your problem is that you're not opening your hips. It's just like golf. You've got to—"

"Don't start on me, Dad. I can't think about anything else. I've got enough stuff going around in my head already." Wilson realized his voice had come out a lot louder than he had intended, and now, everyone was looking at him. But he finished what he had to say. "I'm going to do it my own way. I was hitting fine before everybody started telling me what was wrong with my swing."